Ruby's Story

Holly Schindler

Ruby's Story

Published by InToto Books

Copyright © 2021 by Holly Schindler

This is a work of fiction. Names, characters, places, and incidents are either the product of the author's imagination or are used fictitiously, and are not to be construed as real. Any resemblance to actual persons, living or dead, business establishments, events, or locales is entirely coincidental.

Formatted and designed by Holly Schindler

Cover image by Jaroslaw Grudzinski, courtesy of Shutterstock

Fonts: Borgoforte Script by CallMeStasia and Fipty Serif by Grafontza, both courtesy of Font Bundles

Ruby's Story is the prequel to the
Ruby's Place Christmas Collection:

Christmas at Ruby's
I Remember You
Sentimental Journey
The Gift That Is Ruby's Place

Ruby's Story is also the first of the
Ruby's Regulars series.

Check **HollySchindler.com** for future installments.

1.

1952

NEW YORK, December. The month of dreams. Of pink noses pressed against store windows. Of snowflakes swirling, doing cartwheels between the high-rises. They glimmered in the streetlights, those snowflakes. And in the moment before they dared to land on the heads peering into elaborate, automated display windows, they whispered promises of romance.

Christmas was coming, after all.

But for the first time in three decades, Ruby wasn't with them. She wasn't in London or Paris, either, two cities where she had occasionally found herself performing on the holiday. She was on a train, the hypnotic chugging and rocking nearly lulling her to sleep. Through the window, the moon painted blue streaks on a snow-covered landscape. It was a lonely looking horizon; at this hour on Christmas Eve, most everyone had already arrived at their destination. Butter cookies were being eaten near fireplaces, washed down with eggnog and rum. Presents were being passed out, *me to you*, in warm living rooms. This hour on this date was no place for ice-coated hillsides—or trains.

And yet, here she was. Headed back to the town she had once called home.

She'd left New York on impulse the day before, packing lightly. With no idea where she would stay or even what she would recognize. Putting a pine-festooned Grand Central behind her.

It wasn't a bad way to spend the day before Christmas, really. Trains were still an elegant way to travel. She had twisted her hair in pin curls and nestled comfortably in a Pullman sleeping car; she'd enjoyed four meals in the dining car, delighting in the china plates and the shrimp cocktail and the festive gingerbread and peppermint meringues.

Besides, she had spent her adult life traveling in a manner that others would have called *alone*, no male companion to offer her his arm. She found that to be tunnel-vision; why, she had always been surrounded by people. Members of her dance company or fellow travelers who shared their newspapers or stories to pass the time.

Christmas Eve, though, well...that was another story. There she was, the only person left in the entire car, her face reflected hazily in her window. An empty seat beside her, an empty seat facing her.

Distantly, she became aware that the conductor was making his way down the aisle of her passenger car—the same conductor who had sat with her in the bar car three hours ago, sharing the last of the split pea soup and cheddar toast, all that remained of their night's menu. At an earlier hour that very evening, he'd still been checking tickets and making holiday small talk. At this one, he was simply whistling. It was a kind of random tune, the carols having already been retired for the year.

"Young lady," he announced, as a way to fill the air, "you're cutting it awfully close. Santa may have already completed his Sullivan stop. And here you are, still on the last train, yet to see the Welcome sign."

Ah, yes. Sullivan. The town where she had been a child.

She shifted in her seat, ready for a fresh round of conversation, when the conductor placed a hand on his chest. "My dear," he gasped, "you're hurt."

She wasn't—not any more than she had been when she'd boarded. The skin on her feet was raw, an angry sort of red. Sores had started weeping through some of the bandages she had applied half a country away. She had bright shiny corns on each knuckle, and the nail on her left big toe had turned black.

"I'm sorry—I'm a dancer." She scrambled for her heels. She had slipped them off in the empty train for a little relief.

"That right? What kind of dancer?"

"Ballet."

She saw it—the flicker of disbelief. Understandable, really. She was older—and not, anymore, merely by a dancer's standards. She had enough years under her belt that she had started using Brownatone on the white strands popping up in her chestnut hair.

It had been rather spectacular, actually, that she had danced so long. The girls she'd started out with had retired some ten years ago or more. Really, the only reason she had lasted was because she had consistently lied about her age, at times switching up the number in the same conversation, all to keep anyone from firmly attaching any number to her. And, too, she'd endured by becoming something of an Isadora Duncan, especially the past few years— folding ballet into modern dance, to be performed to small groups of patrons. Well-to-do women, wives of important men who liked to host dinner parties and believe that they were supporting the arts.

But the end of her career was coming, she knew. Faster than this train could travel. Which was maybe why she'd found herself so anxious to get back to the beginning.

The conductor patted her shoulder and offered a crooked smile. Ruby'd seen that smile before—it tickled something in the back of her brain. But she couldn't quite figure out what.

"Not far now," he assured her.

On she rode, the train chugging and pulsing about her. Whistling to announce her arrival.

The station in Sullivan was as she remembered. Except for the fact that it was empty. And that instead of leaving, she was coming.

The smell of the station was also familiar. It was the smell of her father's work shirts, the ones he'd once worn as a railroad mechanic. When a solitary figure appeared, she almost expected him to call her kiddo and insist, "Hurry on, now, your mom'll think we've taken the 7:15 to Hot Springs."

But when the figure stepped out of shadow, she found a stranger, mop in hand, ready to make sure she vacated the area quickly—so that he could lock up. Obviously, hers had been the last train scheduled for the night.

"Sir," she began, "could you tell me where I might find a hotel?"

"You don't have a place to be? You came on Christmas Eve without arrangements?" His face twisted, and Ruby got it again—that funny tickle. His expression was familiar, but why?

The man's voice softened as he admitted, "I'm on my way out. I'll drop you at the Grand. It's about five blocks from here. They should have space."

"Christmas and all," Ruby finished for him.

He flinched, seeming not to want to acknowledge it: a woman, all alone, on Christmas. He offered her a nod.

His car was old, with the rounded fenders she remembered from her childhood. The interior smelled faintly of sweet pipe smoke. Mohair seats.

"Surprised to see an out-of-towner," the man admitted. "Where you from?"

"Here, actually," Ruby said, not wanting to give the other possible answers: New York, Europe. Her feet had taken her all over the world. She had cared for herself, in the same way her cherished namesake aunt had taken care of her most prized treasures—the tissue paper, the gentle ways she had about storing her hair combs or silk stockings. Ruby had never joined the dancers in their cigarettes and their habits with men, their dinners of coffee and cottage cheese to keep their weight down. But even the most cared-for things could not escape time's rough ways. Pages yellowed, celluloid cracked. Women wrinkled. Muscles atrophied. Bodies were meant to start strong and wither.

Ruby petted the seat beneath her. The mohair, she thought with a scowl, had turned bald in places.

"Here?" the man repeated. "In Sullivan?" He leaned into the wheel as he drove, hands clutching the top.

"I grew up here," Ruby said softly, scanning both sides of the street. She recognized no businesses. New signs were like Halloween masks, giving her a hard time making out the shape of the buildings beneath. Had that once been a Woolworths? The café where she had downed hot fudge sundaes with that aunt of hers?

"Me, too," the man said.

The conversation faltered. Ruby was no good at small talk.

The man paused outside of the Grand. Ruby clutched the leather handle of her single bag and started to step out, but paused. "Is this—"

"The site of the old Pendleton place? It is at that."

"Huh. So they—"

"Sold the land to a developer who built the hotel."

"Wow," Ruby moaned.

"There are other hotels with rooms, surely. But I thought you'd prefer this, Ruby," the man said.

She gasped at the sound of her name. Telling him she'd been a hometown girl had helped him recognize her. But who was he?

She turned toward the face in the car. The man wasn't wrinkled or silver-haired; in fact, he wasn't much older than her. Was he? Surely not. When he flashed a playful grin, the pieces clicked. Ruby could remember the boyhood version of this very face pulling her hair on a playground in another life.

"We sure did have some times out there on that pond, didn't we, Ruby? You and me and everybody else in Sullivan."

"We did. Thanks, George," she said.

"Don't mention it, twinkle toes," he said. "Merry Christmas."

"Merry Christmas," she laughed, slamming the door behind her.

"Oh," she tried to call out. "But the pond. Is it still here?"

George didn't hear. He was driving off—to a family or a dog or a church service. Ruby felt foolish for not knowing which. For not asking about him. And how the years had been for him.

Nothing to do now but go inside.

2.

RUBY'S feet hurt. The sound her shoes made against the marble hurt, too. It sounded like a chisel, carving something.

Mostly, it was digging out a hole inside her heart.

"Well, well, well," the desk clerk called out.

Ruby stopped abruptly. The man from the station recognized her. Did this woman? Here she was, Big Time Ruby, come to the end of the line.

And what did a woman do, when at the end?

She goes back home, Ruby thought.

Fancy Ruby. Worldly Ruby. Here, in little Sullivan, Missouri. Looking for a sign.

"A guest!" the clerk exclaimed, throwing her hands into the air. She was an older woman, white-headed with a body like a tiny winter tree with no leaves.

The lobby smelled of pine and the hot cocoa in the woman's teacup.

"I used to love cocoa as a kid," Ruby said, without thinking. "Always with marshmallows. Homemade marshmallows, back then. Made by my aunt's friend." She found herself wishing, distantly, that she had let her (Ida, that had been the friend's name) teach her the recipe. It seemed, looking back, that she had tried a time or two.

"What's that, dear?" the woman asked. She wore a black dress beneath a green cardigan. She had pulled out her best pearl earrings, Ruby thought.

"You look lovely," Ruby told her.

The woman tossed a hand at her. "It's Christmas Eve! You're supposed to wear something special for Christmas. It's nothing compared to what you have on."

Ruby's dress was all but invisible beneath her red wool coat with the black fur cuffs and collar, but the coat was designer, purchased on Fifth Avenue, along with her black kid gloves. Her hair was in its usual bun, showing off her round, gold earrings and red mouth.

Ruby looked like New York, the fashions taking a slower time getting to other areas of the country. The clerk eyed her with envy.

"I thought for a while I'd dressed for myself and the ghosts," the woman admitted.

"Ghosts?" Ruby asked as she tugged off her gloves.

"Oh, just an expression. You come for family?"

Ruby hadn't. They were gone, by then. All of them. Even her parents. Her aunt. Passing far sooner than they should have. But with no one in Sullivan, what had drawn her?

Ruby felt a tingle on the back of her neck. A sign, that was what she'd wanted. Some sign as to what she should do next. Where to go, what to work on.

Would this woman offer it?

"Perhaps you and I could have breakfast tomorrow morning," she simply said.

Ruby nodded, her thoughts elsewhere. There had always been dance, a whole world of people and music and applause. But that was dying on her. Funny—as much as it felt to Ruby that she was aging, it also felt like dance itself was. Dance was liver-spotted and it had a heart condition. Somewhere, a tombstone was being carved with its name on it.

Ruby needed to fill the hole inside her. But with what?

"With what?" she asked the woman, before she could stop herself.

"I was going to make a Swedish tea ring."

Ruby caught herself laughing, though she wasn't immediately sure why. Maybe the idea of a Christmas pastry being all she needed to feel satisfied.

The woman flashed it—the same look that Ruby had seen on the train, and in the station. And it hit her: it was the same look people used to flash Ruby's aunt. An eccentric who had loved sledding and snowball fights as a full-grown woman. Who had never married, who had carried on full-blown conversations with herself in the market. Who had taught Ruby the most important part of dancing—feeling the music, letting it take you over—on the sidewalk of the town square.

It all flooded Ruby suddenly, along with the sureness that *this*, mostly, was why she had come. To get back to it, the way she had felt with her namesake aunt. She needed to return to the lightness of it, of her youth, of not being bothered by the stares.

It sounded like a lie, but it wasn't. When the two Rubys were together, they could laugh at the disapproving looks.

It hit her: she needed that. She needed a serious dose of the *Don't Cares*. An old woman ballerina-slash-modern dancer. The absurdity of it.

Almost as absurd as an aunt teaching her niece how to Charleston down the sidewalk outside the Sullivan bank.

Being here, though—it wasn't working. The looks from George and the hotel clerk hadn't been disapproving. They'd been worried. And they were pinching at all her sore spots, like her shoes pinched at her raw feet.

Maybe, she thought, this was a mistake.

"I gave the last of my dinner leftovers away," the clerk admitted. "But there's a Campbell's soup vending machine just around the corner."

Ruby sighed.

"I'm going to midnight service, if you'd like to join me."

Ruby was certain she looked like someone who needed a spiritual uplift. In fact, she *was* someone in need of a spiritual uplift.

But she wasn't going to find it in a church.

Only one place might work.

"When I was younger, there was a little pond near here," she started. "I was thinking how nice it would be to visit it. Under the moonlight. On Christmas Eve."

"The old Pendleton pond."

"You remember it?"

"Honey, it's still out there. Right behind this very building."

3.

RUBY hugged herself as the galoshes she had tugged on over her heels crunched against the snow. It smelled cold outside. And a little eerie.

"Right out that way, hon," the clerk said, pointing.

"Okay," Ruby said. "I've got it. You don't have to walk with me. It's freezing out here."

"You sure there's nothing I can get you?"

Ruby knew why she had asked. Her eyes were sparkling with tears. But these weren't sad tears. They were happy. So happy. The pond! Still here.

Ruby reached for the woman's hands. "Your name," she told her.

"Aren't you a dear," the woman said. "It's Ethel."

"I'm Ruby."

"Ruby." Still, the clerk showed no sign of

knowing who Ruby was. And Ruby could not place Ethel. Who was she? When had she arrived in Sullivan? All were details to be learned later. Now, Ruby had other things on her mind.

"I'll put your bag behind the desk," Ethel offered. "Other than the traveling salesman and the elderly couple who decided to book a room when their family ran out of guest beds, you're our only occupant. Here's your room key."

Ruby smiled a thank-you.

"You won't stay out here too long, will you, Ruby?" The exchange of names only seemed to make Ethel feel more responsible for her. She squeezed Ruby's chilled fingers, reminding her she'd left her gloves inside in her haste.

"No. I just—I fell in love out here. When I was a girl."

Ethel flashed a look of understanding and let go of Ruby's hands.

Ruby ran, as much as she could run in the drifts of Missouri snow. Her breath shuddered as she caught sight of it: the pond, frozen, frosty and blue beneath the moonlight.

She closed her eyes and she could hear it—the slice of ice skates.

And laughter.

4.

1922

MISSOURI, November. It was a cold month, almost abnormally so. Rust colored leaves should still have been thick on the trees. But there was no color out by the old Pendleton pond. Nothing but the bluish white blanket of snow and the black fingers of tree branches.

Ducks should have still been swimming, their yellow beaks and green necks glimmering wet beneath the sun. But they'd flown off, in their honking V-shaped formation. Instead, the families throughout Sullivan were the only creatures to have formed something of a post-Thanksgiving Day flock, the ice now thick enough to support them all on skates.

They came, the families, after large early afternoon feasts. They came with warm hearts. They came in mittens and woolen skirts. They tightened their laces and they pushed off the bank and they started to glide forward, their mufflers rippling out from the knots beneath their chins.

Ruby knocked at the back door of the sprawling, intimidating old Pendleton place. Her namesake aunt appeared, tugging on her gloves. Ruby took a deep breath, savoring the aroma of toasted marshmallows and warm cocoa. She knew those treats were meant to be ready for all the Pendleton kids, those heaps of grandchildren and cousins and nieces and nephews who had gathered for Thanksgiving. She knew the sweets were meant to fill their bellies up once again after their time out ice skating. But Ruby also knew a portion would be waiting for her, too, as soon as she and her aunt returned to the kitchen door.

"Ida," Ruby's aunt called to the Pendleton cook, "I'll be back for those dishes in a minute."

"You'd better be," Ida started to threaten. "You're the housekeeper, you know, and dishes are your..."

But the door fell on her thin warnings.

"You sure you don't want me to wait while you finish that job in there?" Ruby asked her aunt. "You don't want Ida mad at you."

"Don't you worry about it," her aunt said with a wink. "As I'm always telling Ida, you get rid of enemies only by making them your friends."

"As if Ida would ever be your enemy. You two are thick as thieves. Peas in a pod. Two of a—"

"I didn't mean Ida," her aunt said, placing a finger to her lips and gesturing toward one of the upstairs windows, where old man Pendleton's face could be seen through the glass. The scowl he wore, clear even from that distance, was for the employee cutting out in the middle of the day to play.

The two Rubys ran, their galoshes smashing and crunching into the snow. They raced each other, like children.

And for the most part, the younger Ruby still did consider herself a child. She felt far more affinity for the porcelain-faced dolls in the chest in her bedroom than for the rouge in the small pocketbook that dangled from the knob on her bedroom door. Fourteen—Ruby doubted anyone even meant it when they called her a "young lady." She was a kid.

They raced, giggling. Every so often, her aunt would scoop up a handful of snow, pack it, and toss it at Ruby, as though to try to slow her down.

In turn, Ruby playfully tugged the wool headscarf from her aunt's head, exposing her gray hair to the sharp winter air.

And still, they laughed, their cheeks tingling, as they finally reached the fringes of the pond.

They shared the bench at the water's edge. The same bench the entirety of Sullivan had used, at one point or another. What did it matter that the Pendleton patriarch never came out to the pond, that he glowered when anyone mentioned skating on his land? The fact that he'd had that bench dragged to the pond (a bench he had never once been seen sitting on himself), why, that was proof of how he truly felt about it all. The bench wasn't just a shrug of the shoulders; it was his invitation. *Please come over*, that action proclaimed. And that was what rang in their heads, the families, far louder than any scowl the old man ever wore when his skating pond was mentioned.

Ruby's aunt laced up first, pushing herself off and skating away.

"Hurry up, twinkle toes," George teased as he glided past.

Even then, everyone knew Ruby as a dancer. Winner of the Sullivan Dance Competition the last three years in a row, the one held in the elegant Kemper Ballroom. Anyone who partnered with Ruby was sure to win half of the hundred-dollar prize money.

George, for all his teasing, was making his play to be her partner next year.

Ruby stuck out her tongue.

She quickly knotted the skate and raced to catch up with her aunt.

Not that her aunt even noticed.

She was throwing her arms out in exaggerated motions. Taking long strides. Almost like a regular figure skater.

Ruby dodged, so as not to be whacked in the face by her aunt's hand, and felt her shoelace snap.

She growled in frustration and turned back, heading to the bench.

As she inspected her lace, trying to figure out how to make the shortened portion work, her aunt coasted by, holding one leg out behind her and an arm toward the sky.

Ruby laughed. "You look like a hood ornament," she shouted, which made her aunt chuckle, too. So much so, she wobbled, threatening to lose her balance completely.

A chorus of "Whoa"s and "Look out"s erupted. A few hands reached out to grab hold of her aunt and steady her.

Once her aunt was righted completely, Ruby sighed with relief, putting a hand on her chest.

Turning back toward her skate, she realized a young man had stopped right in front of her.

He smiled, bowed, and began to twirl. When he was finished, he held his arms out from his sides.

Was he, too, trying to audition for the role of her next future dance partner?

No matter—Ruby was feeling warm and giggly and happy. She assumed he was feeling the same, whoever he was. Maybe a relative visiting Sullivan for the holiday?

At any rate, he was surely playing. They all were. *Twinkle toes*. Teases. Winks. Laughter. Why, it would not be hard to imagine that even old grumpy Pendleton himself would show up in a pair of skates to join them. Skates and a cane! It was almost too silly to picture.

And yet…

Ruby smiled, tilted her head to the side, and held her arms out in a similar fashion.

She expected another playful move back.

But the young man—whoever he was—simply dropped his arms, disappointed, and skated off.

5.

RUBY felt bad. Like she had missed something. Like she had hurt the boy's feelings.

She pushed off from the bench and skated as fast as she could, trying to catch up. She searched the faces, pink and smiling. Laughter and voices surrounded her, but it didn't feel warm anymore. The boy had vanished. Had she hurt him that much, that he'd had to leave?

Ruby returned to the pond for the next several days. At times, she found the pond empty. Others, she came upon a young skater or two. A couple holding hands. A group of rowdy little boys, once, in their short pants and their thick socks for the winter, building a ramp that would let them slide across the entirety of the pond.

And then, finally, one day—

"There," Ruby sighed. She cupped her mouth and called out to him to get his attention.

But he only kept on skating, his hands folded behind his back. Was he ignoring her? Was he that angry?

She raced to the bench to change out of her boots. The pond was not exactly empty that particular afternoon, but it wasn't nearly as full as it had been on Thanksgiving. As she struggled with the laces, she waved again. This time, with both hands, over her head.

She had everyone else's attention. Some were giggling—there she went, acting like her don't-care-who-sees-this aunt. Others shook their heads.

As the strange boy rounded the final curve, she did it again: arms over her head, waving desperately.

His whole face brightened at that point. He increased his speed, pumping his arms.

Ruby's heart beat a little faster.

He stopped in front of her. He was handsome, she noticed. The kind of handsome that got turned into paintings.

Before she could think of something to say, he did it again—twirling and swirling about, then holding his arms out from his sides.

This time, Ruby cheered and applauded.

Again, the young man's face drooped in

disappointment. He shook his head at her, lowering his arms and skating away.

~

"TWICE now," Ruby told her aunt as they made their way across the Pendleton field.

"Why do you think I'll know something about it that you don't?" her aunt asked—somewhat dismissively, Ruby thought.

"Because you—" Ruby stopped, feeling a sudden empty space beside her.

She turned, finding her aunt a few steps behind, jumping up repeatedly, attempting to snatch at a tree limb. And jumping out of the way when the snow that had collected on the branch tumbled to the ground.

"Are you listening?" Ruby called out.

"Listening," her aunt affirmed. She dropped her skates, opened her arms, and tilted backward a dangerous amount.

"No—" Ruby started, tossing her own skates to the side and reaching out to her.

But it was too late. Her aunt had fallen on her back.

"Are you okay?" Ruby asked, scrambling after her. By the time she reached her aunt's side, though, she was flapping her arms and legs, making a snow angel.

Ruby frowned. Usually, she adored these antics. They seemed to prove that worrying about the rules of life—the library book due dates and the length of skirts and the lines to sign on and floors to sweep—were the silly things. Being who you wanted to be, indulging in the pleasures that rule-followers seemed so determined to leave behind with the memories of childhood, why, that wasn't silly at all.

Usually. That was usually how Ruby felt.

At that moment?

She frowned and grabbed hold of her aunt's wrist, hauling her up to standing.

They gathered their skates. Ruby didn't bother to dust the snow from her aunt's back—that was a condescending move, something you did for a child. She simply hurried her aunt on, down toward the bench.

As they traded their boots for skates, Ruby surveyed the bodies on the pond.

"What makes you so sure he'll be here today?" her aunt asked.

"Because it's the weekend. Nearly everyone comes on the weekend."

Her aunt hummed "Ain't We Got Fun" as Ruby continued to search the faces.

"There!" Ruby shouted. "There he is."

It happened all over again:

The bright, happy expression washing his face.

Racing toward Ruby.

Swirling in front of her.

Holding his hands out.

Ruby cheering.

The disappointment.

Skating away.

"See?" Ruby squealed. "What is he doing? What does that mean?"

"He's trying to talk to you," her aunt said, pointing to the ice.

When Ruby craned her neck, she realized that he had used the sharp blade of his skate to carve a cursive word into the ice: *Hello*.

Ruby jumped to her feet and raced across the pond, toward the young man.

"Hey!" she shouted, to no avail.

"Hey!"

And still, he skated on, hands lodged deep in his pockets.

"Hey!" She reached forward, touched his arm.

He turned, slowing down a bit once he recognized her.

She pointed toward the edge of the pond. "Let's get out of traffic," she said, but had to put her hands on him to steer him to the side.

"I didn't realize what you were doing," she tried to apologize.

But he only looked at her blankly.

She pushed herself about a foot away from him, and began to swirl her skates across the ice. Clumsily, she wrote:

"Pie?"

6.

RUBY and the young man walked from the Pendleton place toward Main Street.

"That was a clever trick, with the skates," Ruby said.

But the boy only stared straight ahead.

"Thanksgiving was the first time I saw you out at the pond," she tried again. "Are you new to Sullivan?"

Again, nothing.

"You know," Ruby teased, "now that our skates are officially off, we could communicate with actual words."

Instead, he tilted his head back, closing his eyes briefly and breathing deep. He was such a pretty boy—with blond hair and bright blue eyes. He was like an illustration on the cover of a dime store novel. A love story, though, not one of those dark, hardened crime things.

"Frankie's has the very best pie," she offered.

When he still didn't answer, she began to wonder what they were even doing.

"This is it," she grumbled, pointing at the front of the diner.

That time, the young man jumped and lunged toward the door, opening it for her. Smiling as she walked inside.

Frankie nodded once toward Ruby, shaking the rough ends of her finger waves. She was a hardy mountain of a woman, clomping about in her black block heels, breasts swinging inside her blouse—almost like punching bags, Ruby often thought to herself with a tiny chuckle.

Word had it that Frankie's diner was something else completely after dark. That the right password whispered at her back door would get you entry to the best little jazz club in the whole of Missouri. And the best martini, with the best bathtub gin.

A speakeasy.

Ruby didn't know if it was true, but she liked the story.

Frankie paused her rush across the floor to eye Ruby's companion suspiciously—she wore it like a favorite dress, that suspicion. Another reason that Ruby had assumed those rumors about her after-dark life were probably mostly true.

As Frankie watched on, Ruby's companion pulled off his gloves and began to go through his coat. "I like her apple raisin," Ruby blubbered.

Still, he continued to pat the large pockets on his sides.

"Should I get us two slices?"

No response.

Face burning, she held two fingers up toward Frankie. "The usual."

"Grab yourself a table, girlie," Frankie barked. "You know the drill."

Frankie let out a snort of disapproval as Ruby steered the young man toward a table at the front window.

He sat, now sticking his fingers in his coat's interior pockets. The entirety of the diner flinched against the strange, almost wounded sound he made when he finally discovered what he'd been looking for. He removed a small notebook and a pencil. He licked the tip of the pencil and scrawled on the top page, then placed the notebook on their table and slid it toward Ruby.

"It smells like snow outside," he'd written. "Also, I'm deaf."

Ruby wiggled her fingers, wordlessly asking he pass her the pencil. "It smells far better in here," she wrote back. "Also, I'm so glad."

He frowned. Wrote, "Glad?" and passed her the notebook.

"It means you don't think I'm a bore."

He shook his head at her, wrote, "I think you're the most interesting person in Sullivan."

7.

WHEN you have to write your conversations, you wind up cutting quickly to the chase:

"*What is your name?*" she asked, before they were halfway through their slices of pie.

"Timothy. Yours?"

"*Ruby.*"

"Lovely. What is your biggest dream?"

"*To dance. You?*"

"To watch you dance."

She curled her finger, asking him to follow her outside.

She danced. Right there on the sidewalk. As the people of Sullivan watched on, she jumped and she twirled. She pirouetted.

She put on quite a show, right there, as the snow began to fall. She looked like a figure in a snow globe.

By the time she stopped, Timothy's entire face had changed.

Ruby grabbed hold of his notebook. "?" she wrote.

"I never understood music until I saw you dance," he wrote.

"There was no music."

"There never is. But it started playing when you started moving."

8.

THEY became the kind of inseparable that finds the youngest of couples. They loved each other. In a matter of moments. Right there on the sidewalk. Adults like to say it takes time for love to bloom. It's something that needs time to grow.

But that's a lie.

Adults simply don't remember the way it happened for them. They don't remember that real love blooms in seconds. The strongest love isn't something you have to convince yourself to feel. It just *is*. As time goes by, the world chips away at it. Takes bites out. Pulls it off in bits and pieces.

The biggest loves still remain in the end, despite everything.

For Timothy and Ruby, it had nothing to do with looks or some sort of silly school popularity. It had nothing to do with social status.

They saw each other, out there on the sidewalk. They knew each other. And they loved what they knew.

They danced together. It was Ruby's favorite part—they danced in front of Frankie's diner; she taught him steps, and he didn't care that people laughed.

After all, he couldn't hear it.

Ruby had already been taught not to listen to the snickers. Her aunt had been teaching her that lesson for years.

"What you doin' with that boy, anyway?" Frankie growled at her one day.

"Nothing, yet," Ruby said. She wasn't being flippant. She'd meant it literally—Timothy hadn't arrived yet. And she wanted to call attention to the card placed on the small table near the window. The first table they had shared together; the only table she felt certain they would ever share. It had become theirs. Each time they planned to meet at Frankie's, Timothy would come early, leaving behind that card. A small white tent right in front of the chair he always pulled out for her, with "Ruby's Place" written in perfect, elegant cursive.

He'd reserved her seat again that day. *Ruby's Place*. She loved that.

"Don't be smart," Frankie warned.

"What am I doing with Timothy?" Ruby said, repeating Frankie's question. "I plan to eat with him. When he gets here. Hopefully, some of your peppermint cake." Ruby stared into Frankie's disapproving eyes.

Frankie leaned farther over the counter, so close that Ruby could smell the coffee on Frankie's breath. She twisted her mouth into a snarl. "Come clean."

"About?"

"Look, I know his family. He's living with his uncle right now. Robert Ludlow. Owns that garage."

Ruby sighed. "And?"

"Told you, I know the family. Ludlow helped send him to that deaf school, up in some big city. He's just a couple 'a years older than you, but he's as far as he's gonna get, school-wise. He's workin' that garage now. Carryin' a notebook around and writin' everything. That fancy school taught him all that talkin' with his hands, but nobody else knows what he's sayin'. Anyway, he's lucky to have Ludlow. But it's set in stone. He's gonna be workin' there the rest of his life."

"And?" The garage did not seem like a lowly job to Ruby; her family didn't own a car. Timothy had taken her for a spin in Ludlow's Tin Lizzie, and it had felt like flying.

"Look, girlie," Frankie snapped, "I don't like the idea of you runnin' that sweet boy around. Leadin' him on."

"I'm not—"

Frankie glared. Suddenly, Ruby understood: the first time Ruby and Timothy had stepped inside the diner together, Frankie had been suspicious of *her*, not him.

"Why would you think—"

"'Cause you got a ticket out."

Ruby laughed. "My father's a mechanic at the railroad. Nothing fancy. And my aunt cleans up at the Pendleton place. The only tickets we Westbrooks get are for the occasional movie."

She reached for the glass dessert display, turning the wheel to see if Frankie's peppermint cake was, in fact, still available.

Frankie grabbed her wrist. "I'm not playin'."

Ruby felt the skin on the back of her neck tighten. For some reason, Frankie was sounding and acting rougher than usual. Almost menacing. And Frankie Hall was not the kind of woman Sullivan residents dared to take anything but seriously. Rumors swirled. How did she keep that speakeasy of hers safe? Ruby'd heard tell she kept a derringer in her stocking. Wasn't afraid to pull the trigger. She'd seen a couple of holes in a back fender that were supposedly attributed to her.

"I'm not, either," Ruby said, attempting to

squirm out of her grasp.

"Times aren't great," Frankie said. "I know all about that. I know…" Her voice trailed. "…about the extent we can go to keep our heads above water."

Ruby went cold. Even then, she was certain this had to be a reference to Frankie's after-hours business. As the years went by, Ruby would learn that Frankie had told her back-door regulars her diner would have gone under without the speakeasy. And, in these sad tales of woe, Frankie had always cast herself as an innocent with no choice. She'd blamed anything she could on starting that club. First the Farm Depression (since Sullivan was itself still so rural then; even Pendleton had animals on part of his land). Later, it was the fault of the Great Crash of '29. She probably would have blamed it on runs in her stockings or a case of bad canned tomatoes.

Had Frankie really been that hard up? Had the diner really been teetering on the point of collapse? Or was Frankie simply an opportunist, one never to let "a pile of dumb laws," as she'd often referred to Prohibition, stand in the way of a nice profit?

No matter. Right then, that very day, when the two were staring each other down, Frankie was using her speakeasy to needle Ruby about Timothy.

"Times aren't great," Frankie repeated. "And I know how quickly any one of us would leave Sullivan, given the chance."

"I'm not going anywhere," Ruby insisted.

"What'd your mother say when you brought him by?"

Ruby jutted her jaw out.

"Good *night*," Frankie swore. "Haven't even brought him by."

"That doesn't mean—"

"Don't break his heart," Frankie said, in a way that almost sounded like a threat.

When Ruby turned, she realized that Timothy was sitting at their table, looking right at her.

She smiled and waved. "Two peppermint cakes," she said. And headed back toward her reserved seat.

Ruby's Place.

~

AFTER they'd had their fill, Timothy wanted to head back to the pond. At the water's edge, he motioned for Ruby to sit at the bench while he skated to a spot in front of her.

Ruby tilted her head to get a better look at the ice while the blade of his skate carved a new word:

"Go?"

"How did you know?" she signed. She had learned a kind of clumsy version of sign language. But it had been important to her—more than important. Crucial. And she had been a quick study.

"I hear things," he signed back, offering her a smirk. "The story is everywhere. Even Frankie was talking to you about it earlier today."

"How'd you know?"

"What you were talking about looked serious. Far more serious than cream for the coffee. And I don't think you were attempting to rob her," he joked.

Frankie wasn't exactly concerned about Ruby's artistic studies. She didn't even have Ruby's best interests at the top of her mind. It had all been about him, *that* was what Frankie had been grilling her about.

Ruby halfway assumed that Timothy knew as much, but chose to approach the subject differently. Somehow, it seemed, Timothy heard everything. Even what was inside Ruby's heart.

"Your aunt wants to send you. To a dance school," he signed.

"She does."

It had been something of a contentious subject in her home. Aunt Ruby wanted her to go. To study dance. Put her on track to be a professional. But it involved going to a big city, perhaps even bigger than the city where Timothy had himself been educated.

And if even sleepy old Sullivan had Frankie's speakeasy, why, just imagine the kind of trouble that could find a girl (especially a girl on her own) in some sprawling, fast-paced metropolis.

The mere idea of it had aged Ruby's mother. Her hair was thinner. Her skin paler. Her eyes never stopped being round and apprehensive. She had loved her sister's fearlessness, her free spirit, when they were both younger. So much so, she had named her own daughter after her. But now, here, still in the trenches of motherhood, all she wanted was to protect young Ruby. Keep her safe. She wanted a life of comfort and joy for her daughter. To finish high school. Meet a boy. Marry. Be cared for.

If Ruby chased a dream, and it didn't come true, where would she be? Too old to marry, too old to start over.

It was too much of a risk.

But Aunt Ruby, a full decade older than her sister, viewed opportunity as something you didn't shy away from. We each only get one life. Why not peek behind the door, see what's there?

Timothy raised his eyebrows, still waiting for an answer. Bringing Ruby back to the present, the cold bench, his crooked smile.

"I would miss your messages," she said. What she was telling him was, *I can't leave you. How could I?*

We fell in love on the sidewalk outside Frankie's. Earlier, even! The pond. Hadn't we started falling, even then? Weren't we always falling, right from the very start?

Timothy pulled his notebook from his pocket. "I'll write you a letter every day," he scribbled. "I write to you anyway, even when you're right here beside me. What'll be the difference?" When he showed her the paper, he nudged her with his elbow.

"You'll forget me," she signed. "You'll get too busy to write."

"Me? I will never be too busy to write. Your letters will be the most interesting thing in Sullivan."

She tilted her head, telling him wordlessly that it was easy to get busy or forgetful anywhere. Even in simple, quiet old Sullivan.

"You're the one who will forget me," he said. "I'm forgettable. Especially compared to living out lifelong dreams."

"Never." She spelled out the word, forming each letter with a kind of pump of her hand, for emphasis.

"All right, a test," he scrawled. "I will remember to leave you a message tonight. Will you remember to come to the pond first thing tomorrow morning, to see it?"

Ruby smiled.

"Yes."

9.

RUBY thought about sneaking out somewhere around midnight. But she hesitated. What if Timothy hadn't been by the pond yet? Was she supposed to wait for him? In the freezing cold? How long? And if she left early, was she supposed to come back? Could she sneak out twice? Would she be caught, punished? Would he ever be able to believe that she had tried and failed?

And so she waited. He did say first thing in the morning, after all. Maybe he was even planning on coming out near dawn.

When the haziest strips of morning began to filter in through her window, Ruby dressed in her heaviest wool skirt and her galoshes. She unwound the pin curls from her hair, and added color to her lips.

She tiptoed down the hall. Her parents' room

was empty, though.

Voices danced up the stairs.

Ruby followed them, finding her aunt sitting at the kitchen table with her mother. Her father pouring three cups of coffee. The women both turned toward the doorway, to eye her at the same time.

"What?" Ruby asked.

"It's Timothy," her aunt said.

The story unfurled, spilling out onto the cork floor. Timothy had returned to the pond. In the dark of night.

"We don't know why," her mother said. "We don't really know where he was going."

"Skating," her aunt said, as though surprised by her mother's cluelessness.

"In the *middle* of the *night*?" her mother asked. "He had to be taking a shortcut somewhere."

The sisters stared at each other.

"Have you and this boy—been—friendly?" her mother asked, her voice going up at the end in a way that showed her confusion.

"Yes," Ruby said.

"That's what your aunt said. But where—" Her mother stopped herself, sucked in a breath.

The kitchen fell quiet.

What was everyone waiting on? What was left?

"The ice broke," her aunt said. "Pendleton

heard screams. But for some reason, it took him so long to get to the pond."

"Because it didn't sound like a person crying for help," Ruby said. "Timothy's never heard that kind of thing. I bet it sounded to Pendleton like an animal. He went to the barn first."

Her aunt nodded, her eyes distant.

"Timothy's in the hospital, then?" she asked. "I should sit with him."

Her father turned, placing the coffee pot on the burner of the stove.

Ruby felt as though there was suddenly no floor. She was tumbling. Straight into winter's arms.

"He's gone, isn't he?" she asked.

~

RUBY raced outside. She ran to the pond, ignoring the shouts from her family, the pleas to come back.

At the Pendleton place, she fought to catch her breath. There it was, the broken ice. A hole like a wound under the winter sun.

And yet, other sections of the pond, away from the cracks, looked so sturdy.

She sat on the bench, panting, making clouds. Wondering what message Timothy had tried to leave her. She'd give anything to know what he'd wanted to say.

Birds sang. The winter carried on. And Timothy was gone.

But somehow, there, beneath the winter sky, she could still feel him.

"I'll never leave," she said, tears streaming down her cheeks. "I'll never leave you."

And then, inexplicably, right in front of her, a white swirl began to form on the ice. Just like Timothy would draw.

"No," the letters spelled.

"Go."

10.

1952

SHE really had gone. In fact, Ruby had left Sullivan after the holidays. Traveled to New York to study. In light of what had happened to Timothy, her mother had let up on her resistance. Kissed her daughter goodbye. Put her on a train. Sent weekly letters reminding Ruby how nice girls behaved. Ruby's aunt helped fund her schooling—both dance and tutors for the broader high school curriculum, to appease her father. There'd been rent, too, for a room in a woman's boarding house. And tickets to the culture New York provided that Sullivan could not.

And now, here she was, at the end.

She was also faced with a truth as clear as the moonlight: she had returned to Sullivan because she was hoping that maybe, just maybe, she would see another message, as clear as the one she'd seen on the ice. Some tiny little piece of advice that would tell her what to do next.

"Foolish," she scolded herself.

What really was that story with Timothy? *Love*, she'd thought back then. Love? In less than a month? Love? Before their bond had ever been tested? Before there had ever been some commitment?

Her heart had filled with him quickly. But what had she really known of him? And he of her?

He had seen her. He had known where she should be. He had pushed her.

He had taught her about dancing, too. Literally saying something with his feet, with the movements of his body—wasn't that what dance was all about? Wasn't it how she wanted to dance? Hadn't it shaped her career?

Even then, so many years later, after more lasting loves, adult loves, part of her still believed that what had existed between herself and Timothy had been something real. And important. Something she could trust.

But at that moment, there was nothing. No clear message. Only the bluish tint of a Christmas Eve moon on the lonely ice.

The bench wasn't even around anymore.

"But there was probably nothing before," she reminded herself, her breath coming out in cold puffs. "When you saw *go* carved into the ice. It was a trick of the light. Wishful thinking. A broken little girl's heart."

Yes, Ruby thought again, she had imagined the words. Grief-stricken and in shock, she would have considered it cold and selfish to simply race away from the greatest tragedy of her life. She had known, deep down, that she'd never be able to shrug it off, race away, pursue her own dreams like Timothy had never happened. She would have clung to Sullivan, to his memory.

Unless she'd had proof Timothy wouldn't want that.

Unless she'd known that staying would have broken Timothy's heart.

So her own mind had provided the reason. The escape hatch. The excuse to leave.

But she had never left him behind. Even now, standing here next to the frozen pond, remembering him, she could feel him filling up her whole heart.

She pulled herself from the water's edge. Stuck her hands in her pockets. The frigid December air attacked, but she didn't want to go back to the hotel.

Her aunt would have taken a walk.

"Well, then, I'll just take a walk, too," Ruby

decided.

It was a funny time—Christmas morning was yet to arrive, but at that hour, the stillness and the emptiness of the streets made it feel as though it had already passed. The quiet made it feel like everything was over.

No hustle or bustle. No music. No packages. No rumble of cars. No voices. A winter wind whistled between buildings. Somewhere in the distance, a cat. A hollow trash can, rolling.

Ruby finally admitted it: She *was* lonely. So brutally lonely. She had never felt like quite like this, not in any of her previous travels. Her solitude rattled and echoed inside of her.

It was almost too much.

She found herself on Main Street, heading toward Frankie's diner.

Only, it wasn't Frankie's anymore. Frankie was long gone, the building that had housed her diner for sale.

At the plate glass window, Ruby cupped her hands around her eyes, attempting to look inside.

But look at what? Dusty remnants.

The moonlight began to illuminate a spot near the front window. A small table. A two-seater. In front of the chair on the right, a white place card. And the elegant cursive writing: "Ruby's Place."

She gasped. Pressed her face closer to the glass.

"Timothy?" she whispered.

The moonlight died, perhaps concealed by a late-night cloud.

She glanced about the street. When she turned back, for a moment, she saw an image in the glass: the blond hair, the ruddy cheeks, the face of a dime store love story.

"Ti—"

The hazy image vanished.

Ruby raised a hand to her lips. Her eyes tingled. She knew. *For Sale*. She knew.

When this brief intermission ended, the curtain of her life would go up to reveal her next stage was here, right here, right in the town where she had begun. Sullivan.

She would buy this building. What she would turn it into, she didn't know. But it would certainly be something.

Smiling, she touched the cold glass of the front window. And whispered, "Ruby's Place."

Three Years Later...

11.

1955

FALL. Early September. Warm afternoons, crisp nights. The entirety of Sullivan smelled like apples needing picking. Sweaters were being tugged from the drawers where they had been stored. The oppressive summer had given up its hold.

A good time to make big progress on construction. But Ruby was only digging herself another hole.

"It wasn't anchored right," she insisted, pointing at the neon sign that had tumbled from the front of her building onto the sidewalk below.

She said it to quite the audience, as nearly everyone who owned a shop on the same street had burst outside at the sound of the crash.

Lance, owner of Sullivan Sign & Neon, frowned at her, crossing his arms over his chest. "Now,

I warned you that was too much sign," he argued, in that condescending way of his. The one that said he'd tried to explain things to her. Technical things about weight and screws and brick, about wind and the direction her building pointed. Things she just could not get through her head. "Too long, too many letters, and the letters were too big. You trying to pull the whole front of the building off?"

He stared her down, determined not to be liable for the sign now in pieces.

Ruby felt her anger beginning to glow inside of her, a small chunk of burning charcoal beneath her ribcage.

But that anger was not *only* about the sign. It was about the past three years. When she'd first set foot inside the former site of Frankie's diner, the toilets had flushed and the lights had come on. It had seemed a good omen, then, in the early days of her project. She'd have to "bring it up to code," she'd been told. Which had sounded easy enough. Now, that seemed like a euphemism for a near teardown. For figuring out which walls were load-bearing. For rewiring and replumbing. For expanding the kitchen. For creating two bathrooms, each with multiple stalls.

She'd knocked out the drywall separating the old dining area and the former speakeasy. She'd discovered an antique bar tucked into the space. Beautiful, and intricately carved. She had no idea what wood it was made of, only that it seemed to her like a giant box. A hope chest, maybe, or a decades-old trunk, the kind used to store family heirlooms. This particular box, this wooden bar, seemed to her to be filled with the memories of Sullivan.

Convincing her contractors to move the bar—which apparently weighed more than the building and the contents of the storage room combined—had been a heavy-lifting job in itself.

Ruby had succeeded, though; she never would have let that bar go. She'd been surprised to find so much of Frankie's diner still in the old place. Over the years, there'd been a few attempts to bring business back to the building: a bakery, a tobacco shop, among other things. But no one ever stayed long enough to really make use of what Frankie had left behind. (*Or,* Ruby reminded herself, *to demolish it, which is lucky for me.*)

She'd replaced the roof. She had discovered that the floor, which looked good, had wood rot.

Knocking out walls revealed mold. Changing fixtures uncovered still more failing pipes.

And the repairs were delayed and delayed again. Contractors went missing. Permits were postponed. Inspectors never turned up.

Now, Lance and Ruby stared each other down,

both aware that Lance had himself called her installation crew away three days ago, presumably for a bigger job, a better paying job. And Ruby was convinced his rush had resulted in a sign that was not properly anchored above her newly-painted bright green door.

"Why don't you just call it Ruby's?" Lance asked.

Ruby cringed. Because that was not what Timothy had written on the place card. That was why.

But Ruby straightened her back, said, "Why don't you design the sign so that it's more evenly balanced?"

He sighed. "Of course it'd have to be *designed* and *pretty* and have eighty thousand letters. Women do set their eyes on the shiny things, don't they?"

A cold shudder traveled through Ruby. A sick kind of shudder. How did a person even respond to a statement like that?

What Ruby wanted to do was strangle him. Instead, she said, "A circle."

"Say 'gain?"

"Instead of a straight line. *Ruby's. Place,*" she said, moving her hand in two arcs, to illustrate where to put the two words: the top and bottom of a circle.

"Your dime, lady," he said.

"I don't think it is."

But it wasn't Ruby's voice that filled the air

that time. Ruby and Lance both turned to find Walter Drummond, Vice President of the Bank of Sullivan, coming down the sidewalk. Wrinkling his brow at the sight of the damage.

Lance snarled as he picked up the sign's frame. He disappeared into his work truck and took off, leaving the smaller broken pieces behind.

"It's fine, everyone, sorry," Ruby apologized, waving the gathered crowd away.

She toed the remaining glass pieces with her tennis shoe, as though hoping to make it untrue. No one wore tennis shoes in Sullivan, at least not downtown. But Ruby had completely given up her heels. By then, it was tennis shoes and white anklets, everywhere she went. That, and wide-legged pants, almost reminiscent of something that Katharine Hepburn would wear. Khaki and light gray and powder blue in the summer, black and deep brown and navy in the winter.

"Why don't I help you sweep this up, Rubes?" Walter asked.

"Oh, you've got better things to do. I'm a little embarrassed that you heard this particular catastrophe all the way in your office at the bank."

"Now, I'm in need of some good old-fashioned exercise," Walter said, patting his mid-section.

Ruby knew that Walter really wanted a look inside.

And since he was, in fact, her lender, she simply opened the door and ushered him in.

Walter had to step over a few guys still installing plank flooring. Backing up to give them space, he nearly collided into an open, occupied ladder in the middle of the bar.

"Whoa!" came a call from the far side of the room, where contractors were in the midst of securing a mirror behind the bar. They had all seemed to notice how close Walter had come to backing into the ladder at the same time. One let up his grip on the mirror to raise a hand in a *stop* signal. Which in turn made the rest juggle to support the weighty strip of glass.

Walter stopped just before his collision. He swiveled and craned his neck to look up at the two men on the higher rungs of the ladder, attempting to position an elaborate chandelier. But the sound of his dress shoes growing dangerously close, the swing of his arms, his lunge (not to mention the bellow of the men with the mirror) had made the two with the chandelier flinch. Layers of crystal continued to swing, clattering dangerously.

"We got it, we got it," the two assured everyone in the bar.

Hammering and shouting and the whiz of electric saws started in all over again.

"I've got some brooms this way," Ruby told

Walter, pointing toward a hallway that included a storage closet.

But Walter wasn't following.

She retrieved two brooms, two dust pans, a trash can. She was about to tell Walter that only in Sullivan would a bank V.P. offer to help sweep a sidewalk—about to say that really, she should be calling someone to come clean it up properly—but Walter kept her from it.

"Well," he said, his hands locked behind his back, "progress is, in fact, being made. Isn't it?"

It was. That much was true. Plumbing and electric were done. The kitchen was just about put together. But the floors and the drywall in the dining area were still in progress. The painting hadn't even begun. And Ruby desperately needed the furniture she'd purchased (all those tables and chairs and even a piano) to just *get here already*. Not to mention all the dishes and glassware and silverware. The linens. None of that had shown up yet.

Ruby had almost breathed a relieved sigh (*He sees progress!*) when Walter asked, "Would you ever sell?"

"Sell?" Ruby could hardly even get the word out. "Why would I do that?" What she meant was, *Why would you think I'd do that?*

It seemed utterly unimaginable, after everything

they'd gone through. Three years of struggles and fights, of cajoling and following up and never taking no for an answer.

Three years ago, Ruby had put on her best suit—complete with gloves, hat, and heels—in order to appear in front of Walter's desk, requesting a loan. Unheard of, for a woman at that time. But Ruby had arrived in Sullivan with a hundred thousand hard-saved dollars, literally made, she'd often thought, with her blood and sweat. An amount also unheard of for most women at that time. She had already purchased the building outright, and could use it as collateral. Her loan application had been for a small amount, meant to fund her furnishings and a few repairs. It would allow her to put enough of her savings aside to live on while the building was being renovated.

"A no-brainer." That was how Walter had described it at the time. What Ruby'd heard was, *Most men don't come to me with that much capital.*

"Unless," he'd said, "this idea for a business wouldn't fly here. All the money in the world won't fix the wrong location. What is it that you're going to open?"

Ruby'd blanched. All she'd known was that she wanted that building. That part of her still believed she was getting signs from Timothy himself. That this was it, where she was supposed to be for the next chapter of her life.

But what was she doing? All she could see, in her mind's eye, was that chair of hers, the little table for two, the place card. Did she want to open a diner, like Frankie's? A bar, like a legal version of that speakeasy? What? She had asked herself that hundreds of times. Her ideas had waffled back and forth. But now was it, the time to decide.

"A supper club," she'd blurted.

"Supper club? What in the Sam Hill is that?" Walter'd wanted to know.

"We had them in New York. Lovely places. To hear music, eat a nice meal..."

"You got to belong, though? Be a member? A club?"

"Everyone in Sullivan would be welcome. It'd be a place to gather. Not join. No one would ever be excluded."

"Well, we sure don't have anything like that around here." Walter'd frowned, thinking.

"Which means I'd have no real competition," Ruby'd said, her chin lifted and her hands folded in her lap.

"True enough," Walter'd said.

They'd sealed the deal with a handshake and her signature.

No competition, remember? Ruby wanted to tell

Walter as he glanced about the interior of her club. *Why would I sell now?*

"Now, Rubes," Walter told her, reading her face. "You know this renovation has gone on far longer than either one of us anticipated. *Far* longer. You've announced grand openings how many times now? In how many years?"

"But I'm so close."

"You've been close a hundred different times."

"But you think—what? That it'll never get open?"

"I'm a banker, and I think in terms of investments," Walter said. "You've invested a lot here."

"Not just money."

Walter sighed at her in a way that warned her not to get emotional about it. "You've invested a lot," Walter repeated, "but you did get the building for something of a steal, considering it wasn't in the best of shape and had been empty so long. You've done enough work here that there's a profit to be made. You could stop your order on furniture, sell the building; now that it's had repairs, somebody'd be glad to swoop in and—"

"No," Ruby interrupted.

"You should at least consider—"

"No." Ruby shook her head hard enough to feel her chestnut bun working loose. "Don't act like

62

the delays are my fault."

"I wasn't saying that. I was saying there's money here."

"Every permit or request I've ever submitted has gotten put on the bottom of the pile. I've had to ask fifteen times for everything. You know that."

Walter nodded, once, sliding his hands in his pockets. Ruby was getting loud enough that the two men still positioned on the ladder were staring at her.

"How much do you have left, though?" Walter asked quietly. "I heard you left the Grand. That Ethel tried to tell you she'd lower the rent you'd been paying for a long-term room. But you wouldn't hear of it."

"It wasn't right. Everyone has to make a living," Ruby said.

"But why were you staying there, anyway? A hotel? Three years after arriving to town? Why hadn't you found a permanent place?"

"Because Ethel—we have dinner together. Every night. Her husband is gone, so it's just her. We were—it was camaraderie."

"And you left because Ethel is your friend, and you wanted to do right by her, and you *couldn't pay her anymore.*" Walter murmured the last bit at her. "Isn't that why you've been staying upstairs, over this place?"

"The upstairs should be my permanent home," Ruby tried to argue. "Lots of people around here live over their shops."

"But that space was meant to be storage. Doesn't even have a full bath up there, does it?"

Ruby disappeared down a hallway, zipping into a back room being used as an office. A battered desk had been pushed against a far wall and piled with papers. The kind of disorganized mess that could only make sense to one person. Ruby shifted a few envelopes about, finding the forms she had come for.

She snatched the pages and raced back into the main dining room, where she'd left Walter.

"Here!" she called out, moving so quickly that the full legs of her pants swished across her calves. "Here," she repeated once she'd gotten to Walter's side. "Look."

"What is this?" Walter asked.

"I'm submitting my business to be listed in the Sullivan Chamber of Commerce holiday printing. You know, that advertises where in town to buy gifts, where to go for special meals…"

"Are you sure, though, that you'll—"

"Yes," Ruby breathed. "Yes, that's what I'm trying to tell you. I'm so convinced this place will be open well before the holidays that I'm sending my information in for the printing."

"This thing is distributed before Thanksgiving, most years."

"Right. I'll be open," Ruby informed him, "and the phones will be up and running and the kitchen will be humming and music will be playing, and the people of Sullivan will be calling to make reservations."

Walter sucked in a breath. And nodded. "Can't wait, Rubes. You put me down for your first reservation."

"I already did," Ruby announced, walking Walter to the door. "You *and* a guest."

"Ah. I'm required to bring along another customer, am I?"

"Of course. Never underestimate the power of word-of-mouth advertising, masquerading as good old-fashioned gossip."

A bird was singing as they stepped into the afternoon sunlight. A cardinal, from the sound of it. *Pretty, pretty, pretty*...Ruby heard the bird chirping.

"By the way," she said, before Walter was out of earshot, "I've already started placing my liquor orders. What's your drink?"

"Scotch neat."

"I'll have a bottle of Johnnie Walker waiting for you with your name on it."

"Oh, yeah? Red bow and everything?"

"Nothing less!"

Walter laughed, offering a quick wave before heading back to the bank.

Ruby inhaled a deep breath of September as her eyes trailed across the storefronts down her side of the street: the bank; the craft store, with cross-stitched messages on pillow tops; a women's hat store; a tailor; a florist; a sandwich shop; beauty salon; barbershop. The shoeshine stand, where men read newspapers while getting their wingtips buffed. Ruby could even make out the glass globes atop the gas pumps at the Mobil station on the corner.

She felt bad, because the rest of the storefronts were painted and intact and operating and looking good. Ruby'd been there for the past three years with cones in the street, upsetting and interrupting the flow of traffic.

Of course everyone had been concerned about the sound of the latest crash. They had all wanted to know what obstacle she was putting in their way this time. What they'd have to drive around. What would block their own deliveries. What would potentially divert customers away from their doors.

Ruby's eyes pulled away from the gas station, coming back down the line of businesses on the opposite side of the street. She passed the stationery shop and the bookstore, coming to rest on Weber Electronics. Arguably the busiest store in town.

Behind her, the door flew open. "Watch out!" came the shout of one of her contractors.

She stepped to the side as his push broom began to attack the remnants of the broken sign, sending a few shards scattering.

"Watch out!" he shouted again, just as Ruby raised her eyes back toward the electronics store.

The words continued to ring in her ears as she watched Roy Weber step outside his shop, fish his pack of Pall Malls from his shirt pocket.

"Watch out!"

And there he stood, Roy Weber. Smirking at her, it seemed.

12.

RUBY wished she could sweep up the way Roy's sneer made her feel. Wished she could scoop her unsteadiness into the same dust pan that was currently scooping up the last of the splintered glass tubing from her sign. Wished she could toss it.

The closest she could come was retrieving her broom and helping her contractor. But sweeping up shattered bits of her name didn't help her feel any better. In fact, it made her feel worse. Disposable. Breakable.

She was still feeling off-kilter, the heat of embarrassment creeping around her neck, as she stepped back inside.

The door burst open behind her.

Ruby swiveled slowly, expecting to find one of her contractors or maybe, now that Walter was gone,

Lance, back to assure her he was not paying for a new sign, no matter what Walter said. Probably, someone was dragging wet concrete on the soles of their shoes. Or smearing spackle all over her light fixtures. Maybe coming to tell her something else was broken or late.

Instead, she saw a heavyset woman. Kind of squat. Feet turned out in a way that said she had been working on them the entirety of her adult life.

"Hey, there," Ruby said. And because the woman looked what could only be called *beat*, Ruby offered, "Get you something to drink?"

In truth, this was something of a marvelous question. And not just because Ruby's was clearly not open yet. It was, after all, still the era of separate race water fountains.

The woman looked around, slammed her hands on her hips. "Looks like the only drink I'd get in this joint is a cup of sawdust."

That was all it took. Ruby instantly burst into laughter. It was a laughter of relief.

Still, the men on the ladders—or with their knees on the floor—or reaching for another nail— all eyed Ruby with their own version of disdain or disapproval or uncertainty.

"This place used to be a speakeasy," the woman said as she followed Ruby to the bar.

"So I hear," Ruby said, glancing about. None of

her furniture had arrived, not a single piece. So instead of a bar stool, Ruby dragged a stepladder up to the bar. And made a flourish, as though to reveal that the seat was something more than a piece of construction equipment. As though to ask the woman to pretend that it was actually some sort of throne.

Now it was the woman's turn to laugh.

Ruby eyed her a moment, trying to guess her age. When she decided the task was impossible (the woman could have been her own age, five years younger, or twice as old), Ruby announced, "I picked up a few bottles from the liquor store off the interstate. No big orders, just trying out a few recipes."

She zipped toward the kitchen, coming back with a couple of bottles of clear liquid. "I've been itching to do this for someone else," Ruby admitted. "I'm going to be open before Thanksgiving."

"You sure about that?" the woman asked, attempting to squirm into a more comfortable position.

"Of course."

"And the walls aren't painted?"

"It'll get done," Ruby said.

The woman cocked her head. "The holidays are such a strange time," she muttered. "Every year, seems all I can do is look back and think of all the people I've lost. Kind of makes a soul feel like one of those bottles of yours. The more you visit it, the less you realize you've got."

Ruby froze. That was exactly how she felt. She needed to prove to Walter that her business wasn't a lost cause. But she also couldn't stand yet another Christmas alone. She'd already spent the past three mostly by herself. A dinner or Christmas Eve service with Ethel couldn't fill her up, not the way she really needed.

Last year, the lonesomeness had weighed on her so much, she'd purchased a pair of ice skates. Spent Christmas Eve on the pond behind the Grand, telling herself she didn't even care if she fell through.

"Well, you'd better get to it," the woman said, pointing at Ruby's bottles.

Ruby mixed her drink, adding a slice of lime. "Sorry I don't have a better glass," she said, sliding one of the mismatched water glasses she'd been using for her lunch hours across the bar.

The woman sniffed, sipped, and spat the drink out. "Good night, that's bad."

Ruby slumped. "It can't be."

"Well, it is."

Ruby just stared.

"Oh, don't you go looking at me with those pleading eyes. Poor pitiful you. Somebody needs to come rescue you, but it's not gonna be me."

"I have a feeling Frankie may have taught you a

thing or two about mixing drinks. Made out of rotgut liquor. And yet, they were delicious. In fact, she may have used that phrase a time or two on me: 'Good night.' That's a Frankie phrase."

"Nonsense! I always could mix a better drink than that Frankie Hall. She never did listen to me, though. She preferred them strong, not sweet, like I make. She might've liked this awful thing you just served me. Yes, we had many a tussle over it. And 'good night,' that's my phrase. She got it from me. But how could you know? You never did come in Frankie's through the back door, did you, Ruby?" The woman winked.

"How'd you know that was my name?"

"Well, now, folks talk. Besides, that sign was hanging up a good three days before it disappeared. What happened to it, anyway?"

"It wasn't anchored right," Ruby said, her voice distant as she searched the woman's face.

"What, you or the sign?"

Ruby winced at the amount of understanding in that statement. "The sign's not the reason you knew my name, though."

"I might've known the other Ruby."

"My aunt?" Ruby squinted. "Are you Ida?"

The woman smirked.

"It's you!" Ruby came out from behind the bar

to hug her. "Are you still with the Pendletons?"

Ida laughed. "I'm not *with* them, but I sure have been feeding their faces for a whole lotta years."

"Old man Pendleton must be gone ages by now."

"Working for his granddaughter and her family. Those Pendletons just kind of keep passing me on, one generation to the next. I feel like part of their inheritance." She chuckled.

"Still working," Ruby repeated, staring at Ida's white hair as she tried to do the math. Hadn't she always seemed even older than Ruby's aunt?

"What, you think I've got some fancy retirement waiting on me? Shoot. Anyway, what would I do with myself if I wasn't working? Go to more teas at the ladies auxiliary?"

"Pay you twice what the Pendleton grandkids are paying," Ruby offered.

"For what?"

"I need your help. I grew up all around that Pendleton place. You know that. You don't just remember a few cocktails from Frankie. You're an amazing cook. I'm telling you, I need you."

"Yeah, for about a week, before you go belly up."

Ruby stared her round face down seriously. "I need you."

Ida sighed. "I knew I'd be opening about a hundred cans of worms by walking in here. I'll do it. But not for the money. Because I want to be part of it. Your aunt was—she was good to me once. When it mattered. This matters."

"She was good to *you*?" Ruby asked.

Ida cocked her head. "She told you it was the other way around. She said I saved *her* life, didn't she?"

"Yes."

"Eh, she was a liar."

"No, she wasn't."

Ida shrugged.

"Maybe someday I'll earn that story."

"Maybe." And with that, she stood.

"You didn't finish your drink."

"Nobody else is gonna finish your drinks, either."

"I remember your marshmallows," Ruby blurted. "Homemade. And that cocoa."

"I remember you stuffing your face with my marshmallows those winters when you were a girl," Ida said, a light entering her eyes as she settled back onto her stepladder. "Back when we were all a little younger," she said softly. "Before..." Her voice trailed.

Ruby wasn't sure what Ida was thinking of, what she visited in her own mind when she thought of *before*, but Ruby was herself now thinking of Timothy.

For a moment, she thought of saying something about him. But what? Feeling him near? Seeing his face in the glass seemed too close, too personal. It was hers, whatever she had seen. But it also seemed like something that could crumble just from the weight of being spoken out loud.

"It'll be the perfect time for your marshmallows and cocoa," Ruby said instead. "Since I'm opening this fall. They taste so good during the holidays."

"At a bar, though?" Ida asked, her voice getting squeaky at the end of her sentence.

"Not a bar. A supper club."

"A what?"

"You know, a nice fancy place to wear your very best. Eat a nice meal. Listen to some good music."

"High-class."

"Yeah."

"That sounds wonderful! But you've got to tell people what it is. You can't expect them to just know. Around here, folks think supper is a bowl of cornbread and beans. Supper's something granddad ate before heading out to the fields; that's what they'll tell you. Not one of them'll think that it sounds like something you'd dress up for."

"That's probably right," Ruby murmured, thinking of her first meeting with Walter at the bank. *What in the Sam Hill is that?* he'd asked her.

"Well, I'll be here," Ida said. "After my shift tomorrow evening and every day it takes to get you ready. Be here when you open, too. But I won't quit the Pendletons, not after all these years, not until I know for sure that I've got something else just as permanent waiting on me."

"I'm honored to have you, Ida. I'll take any scrap of time you can spare. I'll pay you for your time tomorrow, too."

As though she had the money for that. But this was Ida. Ruby'd just do without somewhere else.

"You need to take on a few other jobs, too, you know."

"Like what?" Ruby frowned as Ida pushed herself from her stepladder.

"You've got to reintroduce yourself."

"To who?"

"To Sullivan. Nobody around here knows you. Or they don't believe they know you, anyway. You've got to show them they do. Same old Rubes." She started to pull away from the bar. The afternoon sun streamed through a nearby window, falling on her face. "Will you do it?"

Ruby nodded.

"Good. I'll be back to teach you the first drink tomorrow. Oh, and Ruby?"

"Yeah?" Ruby paused, the bottles of clear liquor

cradled in the crook of her arm.

"Do yourself a favor. Start by introducing yourself to your neighbor across the street here. Roy. Roy Weber."

13.

ROY WEBER. Sole proprietor of Weber Electronics. That store of his was a regular hub of activity in Sullivan, as the residents were constantly streaming inside, having decided to make the leap into television and rock and roll. An electronics store was a doorway to the future, after all, offering gleaming technology that would open into who-knew-what. An adventure that only required you to plug the cord into the electric socket.

Roy sold Emerson televisions, in stylish wooden consoles. He sold 8mm cameras to create home movies, and the movie projectors to play them on. Brownie cameras to record the important days in life. Clock radios, TV lamps, hi-fidelity equipment.

He was also Sullivan's leading citizen. Seat on the city council. Head of the chamber of commerce.

Deacon of Sullivan's largest Christian congregation. A Shriner and, of course, in charge of the organization's charitable outreach. He marched in every parade. He attended every ice cream social in the summer. He was the master of ceremonies of the annual Christmas tree lighting right there on the square, which usually occurred in the midst of the first snowfall of the season.

He had married old man Pendelton's granddaughter, the same who had inherited a small fortune (and Ida, apparently), a fortune that had only grown when they'd sold the Pendleton land to the developer who'd put up the Grand hotel. And together, they were parents to Sullivan's most obnoxious fraternal twins. But because of Roy's place in town, the twins were referred to (through somewhat strained smiles, Ruby had often noted) as "enthusiastic" or "energetic."

Ruby knew Ida was right. She needed to go over there. Extend a handshake toward Roy. But she still hesitated.

She'd only had one interaction with Roy, and even then, it wasn't much of one. Shortly after arriving in Sullivan, she'd stepped inside his shop, looking for a record player. But Roy had been too busy with another customer. A couple, actually. Probably newly married. Probably arriving to fill an entire newly-purchased home with equally new gadgets.

Too preoccupied to think much of it, she'd

shrugged and headed out for the real chore of the day—driving to the next town over to purchase all the latest, greatest necessities for her industrial kitchen: dish sinks, stoves, grease traps, and all. On the way back, she'd wandered into Jake's Appliances and picked up a Motorola clock radio for herself.

It didn't let her play her own records, but there was a decent classical music station she could tune in. Plenty good enough.

"Weber Electronics," her clock radio barked during ad breaks in her favorite programs. "Lowest prices anywhere. Ask for honest Roy, the fairest guy in town." Maybe all that was true, but she didn't want to go back to Weber Electronics. There was just something cold and uninviting about it.

Best to start with easier outings.

The day after receiving Ida's advice, Ruby smiled at her contractors, slipped into the sunshine, and quickly stumbled upon this truth:

If you lived in Sullivan in December of 1955, there were certain things you knew. The drug store made the best ham salad sandwich, work was plentiful, gloves and hats should always be worn when shopping downtown, a person of respect was always called "sir" or "ma'am," and that woman who moved into Frankie's old diner was an outsider.

New Yorker. Fancy dancer. That was the story.

If there was one thing Sullivan did not need, it was some hoity-toity, uptight restaurant that sold bits of fish better used as fishing bait.

Until Ruby started sticking out her hand. "Ruby Westbrook," she would tell them. "I grew up here."

Only, she didn't tell them like that. Not in those words exactly. She told them with stories. Of her father the railroad mechanic, and how he always smelled of adventure. Of her aunt the free spirit. Of how she'd had her very first dance lessons right there in Sullivan. How the town had been the foundation of everything.

Ida returned that night, as promised. "You sure have been making the rounds today," she observed, unwinding her scarf from her throat.

"You said introduce myself."

Ida snorted a laugh. "Didn't think you'd throw yourself into it with such enthusiasm."

"I practiced at the barre until my toenails fell off," Ruby said.

"And a few toes, I'd wager," Ida teased. "Now, you're going to practice in *this* bar," she added, pushing Ruby toward the kitchen.

"But is it working?" Ruby asked.

"Yes," Ida agreed, "yes, I believe it is."

"How do you know?" Ruby asked as Ida began

banging pots, clearly searching for something that could be used as a double boiler for her from-scratch cocoa recipe.

"I hear. You can't *not* hear in this town. You seen your neighbor yet?"

"Not yet," Ruby admitted. But she assumed Ida knew that.

Determined to make Weber's her first stop the next morning, she barged out of her front door, took two steps off the curb, and felt nothing but negative energy bleeding out from his shop.

But it wasn't as though Weber's was the only place Ruby had left to visit. Why, she'd only been at this introduction business one day! She started in where she left off the day before: Millie's Craft Store. She purchased pillows stitched with the saying "Cardinals appear when angels are near." Ruby talked up none other than Millie herself, telling her those pillows were going to add just the perfect touch to her new living room. And yes, that living room *was* over the place she was opening. And no, no, it wasn't bound to be *just* a bar. Why, it was going to be every bit as elegant as the Copacabana! But don't you worry about feeling uncomfortable. Never happen, not at any place of Ruby's. Why, her aunt would have had her hide if she put together a pretentious place. Things should be special, not pompous. And the kids! The kids were going to love it. You just wait till they get a whiff of my homemade marshmallows.

She went to the beauty salon for the first time since she'd set foot in Sullivan. So hard to pick a new hairstyle, she admitted, settling into the styling chair. She'd worn her hair in a bun so long, it sort of seemed part of her now. An extra appendage. But it sure would be nice if it were cut in such a way that she could choose to wear it down. Imagine coming in and getting her hair set on a regular basis! Why, that would make her feel like royalty. And no, no, there weren't any fancier beauty salons in New York. Any woman on the island of Manhattan would love to get the full treatment in a place like this! A deal if I come in every week? Now, only if you let me match that with a deal of my own. Your first round on me. You'll be there, won't you?

She sat at the counter of the diner down the street, telling the waitresses about the hot fudge sundaes she'd once shared with her aunt. Asking any of them with a bit of age to remember her aunt, the two of them dancing on the sidewalks just outside. Asking the younger sort to imagine feeling that free. Didn't you have a relative of your own, just like my aunt? Didn't you love that person with every pump of your heart? Love them in the sort of whole-hearted way only the youngest and most sincere of children can?

Yes, she was the same old Ruby. Travel and stages hadn't changed her any. She hadn't come to show the poor, backward residents of Missouri that she knew how to be classy, and they all needed her refining. No, she was Ruby, who loved Sullivan. Maybe not exactly the same way she'd loved her aunt, that was its own special thing. But Ruby had loved Sullivan with that same pure little girl heart of hers.

And she loved it still.

This older Ruby, the one chatting up her neighbors, insisted that with age came the wisdom to recognize just how special Sullivan really was. When her retirement arrived, she'd wanted to give Sullivan something special back. Use her savings, painstakingly acquired over decades of hard work, to provide something extravagant and lovely to the people her mind kept drifting back to, fondly. Offer a treat to those who had treated her so well, growing up.

The thing was, it was also true. Ruby realized she believed it, the more she said it. This wasn't only about her next chapter. Not anymore.

Could Timothy have known this would happen?

She couldn't dwell on the possibility too long. Not when she needed to take her shoes to be resoled. When she needed to start frequenting the candy shop.

Suddenly, the woman who had been holed up

in her building the past three years had all the time in the world to talk. But the people of Sullivan didn't begrudge her the time it took her to get here, to this place of smiles and greetings and stories. They were just glad to see her here now.

They asked how things were going. They were interested, now that she had shown interest in them. They started asking about that club of hers. *What is that thing, anyway?* Proving Ida was right, time and time again. They really did need to be told. *Supper club.* If first hearing the words didn't bring confusion, it conjured fear: there'd been a club of sorts there already. That speakeasy of Frankie's, site to one of the worst Christmas Eves in Sullivan history. A regular shootout, or so the stories went.

But Ruby was quick to put other images in their heads, adding only enough detail to make them curious. Because curiosity was like hunger, really. It couldn't be ignored. It would draw them all out.

As days grew colder, the trees redder, and the calendar edged its way into November, Ruby headed out to the church bazaar. Hands raised and fingers wiggled in greeting. Ruby nodded and waved back. She smiled. She browsed the tables. She bought knickknacks and arrangements of dried flowers and some homemade apple butter. Everyone suddenly had something to contribute to Ruby's forthcoming opening. Including, even, a door hanger made of silver bells.

"Might be jumping the gun a little bit," Joanie Wilbury said, somewhat apologetically.

"But it's going to look gorgeous on my door," Ruby said. "I have to have it. I've been looking for something festive for the holiday season. This is perfect."

And it really was. Ruby recalled thinking, when Ida's suggestion was still ringing fresh in her ears, that there was a chance she would edge her way into the Sullivan community and feel only the differences. It was, perhaps, what had kept her so relatively isolated the past three years. But the opposite had been true— she had loved it. Every moment. Every laugh. Because for every story she shared with a Sullivan resident, they shared one with her.

Moving those stories into her heart had made her feel as though she'd officially come home.

Thank you, Timothy, she'd found herself murmuring on a regular basis, turning her lights out for the night. She found herself thinking it again as she turned the silver bell door hanger over in her hands.

"Hey, there, twinkle toes," she heard from the other side of the room. "You gonna buy some of our fresh, genuine honey?"

"Oh, George, leave the poor woman alone,"

came a call from Ruby's side.

"Actually, I'd love some of that, George," Ruby shouted. "Save me two jars."

Maybe, she thought, *Ida can use it in a drink.*

But first, she needed to spend some time here with whoever it was who had just called out to George. "I'm Ruby," she offered, thinking she must have said her own name about a thousand times over the past couple of weeks.

"Betty." Ruby guessed the woman was as much as ten years younger than she was. She could have just stepped out of the pages of *Look* magazine, wearing heels and pearls and a voluminous crinoline underneath her polished cotton skirt. She smiled, surrounded by cellophane-wrapped bundles of cookies.

"These wouldn't happen to be chocolate chip, would they?"

"Gingersnaps," Betty said.

"Even better."

"My husband thinks so. You've probably met him. His store is right across the street from you. Roy? Roy Weber?"

Ruby fought a sudden chill.

"Wish he were here to say hello. He's back at the shop, working up a storm," Betty went on, gathering up a few bundles of her cookies.

At least he wasn't in the room. Somehow, Ruby

wasn't prepared for that.

"My brother's with him. Roy lets Nick work during the holiday season, take home his commission. Even though he works nights in the Chevrolet plant. Poor guy. Been living on about two hours sleep, it seems lately. But he's helping Roy out now, a little earlier in the year, because business has been so good lately. Booming, actually." The way she said it was almost plastic. Forced. Ruby wasn't sure if she was stretching the truth or didn't really want to talk to her.

"You've probably seen Nick," Betty said. "He and Roy, they sure do love their Pall Malls. I keep trying to get him to cut back. Those two must take about fifty cigarette breaks a day. It taints the smell of all the laundry." She paused to grimace. "They sure have seen you. Been watching all the exciting developments on your side of the street."

Ruby nodded, still feeling unsure.

"Been seeing our girl come visit you quite a bit in the afternoons."

"Your girl?"

"I'm sorry, I should introduce myself a little better. Pendleton's my maiden name."

"Ida," Ruby said. "Of course. I don't know why that didn't click right away. My Aunt Ruby used to work for your grandfather. I spent lots of time out there at the old place. Skating on the pond."

"Did you? I was too little to skate on it myself. Some sort of tragedy out there made Grandfather send everyone away." Betty offered a cloyingly sweet smile, returning the conversation back to Ida. "Nothing wrong with visiting an old friend, is there? Once the workday's done."

"It's been good to catch up with her."

The two women stared each other down. Ruby didn't know why she held tight to the truth of what Ida was really doing for her, behind the bar. A need to protect Ida, sure. But a need to protect herself as well.

Why, though?

In that moment, Betty felt almost insidious. Dangerous. Her red mouth stretched into a smile. "You ask me, the only reason those two boys know anything about Ida is because they were staring at your car. Sitting out front of your store. A Studebaker, isn't it?"

Ruby nodded.

"Did you—" Betty tugged at her necklace, her eyes darting back and forth. "—drive yourself today?" She asked in a whisper, her fingers cupped to hide her mouth.

"Sure."

"Ooooh," Betty said, touching her chest. "I can't imagine. You trust yourself to get up that fast? Do you go on the highway?"

"Of course."

Betty blanched.

"You could do it. You'd be fine. It doesn't even feel like you're going that fast. No more so than when you're in the passenger seat." Ruby's voice trailed as Betty started staring at her legs.

"Pants," Betty sighed, shaking her head.

"Come again?"

"What I wouldn't give to go out in pants. And tennis shoes!"

"Why don't you?" Ruby asked. "I bought them over at Graham's Department Store. Elizabeth, over in women's clothing, has been so helpful. She can put together anything and make it look fantastic."

"Oh, no," Betty contended, shaking her head. "I couldn't do it. But I admire your fearlessness, dear."

"I'm not sure trousers and tennis shoes are exactly fearless," Ruby said. "I did damage to my feet after so many years dancing. I don't think I could get back in a pair of heels at this point if I tried. I used to tough it out, but I just can't anymore. And as for the pants, in my days of dance, I learned quick if you kicked your leg up too high..." Ruby started to illustrate by lifting her right leg, "...you could show *all* your secrets to the world."

Betty shrieked a laugh. "You're too much," she said, handing Ruby her cookies and taking her money in exchange.

Ruby shook her head at herself. What was so dangerous about this? A woman who was afraid of the driver's seat! And pants!

Ruby began to breathe a little easier. But she also knew there could be no more foot-dragging. Not now that she had met Roy's wife. Visiting every business in town, then coming home to her own place on the opposite side of the street, without approaching him, well, that looked like straight-up avoidance.

Which, Ruby supposed, it actually had been.

A couple of days after the bazaar, a cloud of paint fumes following her every move, Ruby stuck her face in the front window. Roy emerged from his shop, Nick on his heels. The sunlight glimmered on a gold lighter passed between the two men. Curls of smoke danced about their heads.

They talked, staring at her entrance.

Go, Ruby told herself. Still, she could not stop wishing her feet could glue themselves to the ground or that a contractor could call to her over the strains of the portable radio she'd told them it would be fine to bring, needing her consultation on some unforeseen paint calamity.

What could be so bad about it? Why can you talk to everyone else and not him?

She emerged, finally, waving at them.

"Gentlemen," she greeted as she arrived on the opposite side of the street, extending her hand.

"I'd better..." Nick said, disappearing behind the entrance of Weber's shop.

"I met your wife last weekend," Ruby tried. "I think I ate up all your gingersnaps."

But Roy grunted, raising his cigarette to his lips. "I'd ask you inside, too," he said, gesturing toward the door that had swallowed Nick. "But the women who come in are usually dressed properly." He glared at her pants.

As Ruby struggled to get hold of her thoughts, Roy pressed on, "What do you want to come over here for, anyway? You and that radio of yours. I hear it every morning, you know. Blaring that highfalutin music of yours. Shoving it in my face, that you're not using anything I sold. Stuck your nose up at what I had, all so you could buy from someone else."

"But you were busy the day I tried to buy a record player—I—"

"You going to leave your car parked where everyone can see it? Woman driving a car." He shook his head. "You got any family around to be embarrassed at what you've been doing out here?"

Ruby hurried away, her heart a slamming door. She was furious, suddenly. Angry at the way he'd talked to her. Angry at herself for letting it happen. Had she suspected he felt this way, all along? Is that why she hadn't wanted to visit him? And how could she have misunderstood Betty? She should have considered right from the start that Betty was being a mirror, reflecting what her husband believed.

When Ruby stomped inside her building, she realized one of her contractors had turned their radio up even louder.

"Roy Weber," the voice boomed on the ad—sarcastically, now, it seemed to Ruby—"the fairest guy in town."

14.

RUBY knew it wasn't the smell of marshmallows that brought the two men out of Weber Electronics time and time again. And it wasn't really their Pall Malls, either. It was her. Her contractors. Her painters. Her deliverymen.

She decided to parade about in front of her building, swinging her door decoration, those bells, calling attention to herself. Flaunting the progress she was making in spite of them.

Her linens had already been delivered. And her liquor. Her silver. Her dishes. The painters finished. Her floors were laid. The tile was completed in her restrooms. Her piano had been heaved a scooted into its proper place.

Her sign was finished and delivered, though not installed. At five feet tall, it could easily slip in through the front door. Ruby had it placed against a far wall, roped off. The tables and chairs set up a good distance from it. This time around, she'd requested Lance appoint a double-sized crew from the neon company to install the sign. Under her watch.

Ruby continued to circulate amongst the people of Sullivan. Easier to do now that the town was enmeshed in decorating the square. They were all coming to her—or the street right in front of her building, at least. With Thanksgiving growing ever closer, the high school senior class set up the tree and strung lights, readying for the official lighting ceremony. City council hired its annual work crew to install the aluminum stars: monstrosities (they had to be two feet tall, maybe three) that hung from the lampposts all down Sullivan's busiest commercial stretch. Shopkeepers were outside more than usual, dusting off plastic rosy-cheeked Santas for their doorways, plastering candy canes on their front windows.

With so much activity right beyond her front door, Ruby slipped into her coat and tied on her favorite muffler, racing to be part of it all. She clapped in approval of tinsel on an entrance. She helped the bookstore owner attach a wreath to the sandwich board on the sidewalk, making sure to ask about his daughter, set to come visit for his birthday. She waved at the police officer who had begun to whistle a few carols here and there, and at George as he drove by on his way to work at the train station.

At this point, though, the stories that Ruby told the shop owners or the waitresses or the hairdresser or the man who shined her shoes (she'd traded her tennis shoes for loafers in order to introduce herself) were all taking a different turn. She wasn't just reminiscing. She was flat-out inviting—and these invitations were attached to a specific time and date.

"Soft opening?" Ethel and her mail carrier and Walter asked. "What is it?" the owner of the stationery store and the tailor wanted to know. They'd never had such a thing themselves. Just cut the ribbon, opened their front door, and let the people of Sullivan stream inside.

"I'm trying it all out," Ruby said. "I'll show you what the entire holiday experience will be. What I'll serve, what the ambiance is like. Absolutely no charge. I want to show you so that you'll be able to tell your own customers. I'm open for Christmas parties, for holiday gatherings. Family get-togethers. If my place can bring more traffic to the area, we'll all benefit. And if I can help your business in any way, just let me know."

Millie at the craft store took her up on it, creating displays for each of Ruby's tables, complete with pine sprigs and tea candles. And the owner of the music shop supplied Ruby with all the Christmas-themed sheet music she could have ever asked for. In return, Ruby agreed to include coupons inside her menus, each of which gave credit to the shops for their offerings, as well as discounts on next visits.

A community; that's what Ruby felt she'd created, as much as she'd created a business.

She couldn't wait for Walter to see it. *A sure thing*, he'd called it at the very beginning.

Now, he'd shake off all his doubt and fully believe his own words.

The night of her soft opening, Ruby dressed in a velvet gown she'd purchased from Graham's Department Store. She placed a gardenia in her hair she'd purchased from Lilly's Floral. She welcomed Ida with a warm hug.

"I brought you this," Ida said, pressing a tissue-wrapped box into Ruby's hands.

"You being here is a gift," Ruby tried to protest, pushing the box back. But Ida was insistent. The kind of insistent that meant Ruby sighed, untying the red grosgrain ribbon.

"It's a scrapbook," Ruby said, removing the book and placing the emptied box on the bar. When she opened the tattered cover, she found pictures of herself as a little girl, dressed in her first leotard and pointe shoes.

"Your aunt kept it," Ida said, as Ruby began to turn the pages, finding her younger pictures giving way to newspaper clippings.

"My entire career is here," Ruby said. "But how—"

"I may have continued to keep up through the last years, after she passed," Ida said.

Ruby's heart melted a bit. "Ida, I—"

But Ida took the scrapbook back, before Ruby had a chance to thank her. She flipped to the end of the clips, showing her the blank pages that followed.

"Plenty of space left for all that comes next," she said. "You'd better stick something in there from this soft opening. A napkin, maybe, or a label from one of your bottles. Enough pages here to take you through another five years at least."

Ruby's eyes tingled as she hugged Ida again. "Thank you," she said, grateful not just for the scrapbook and for the proof that her aunt had remained proud until the end of her life, but for Ida's vote of confidence.

Yes, Ruby told herself, *this is the beginning of a long, long chapter.*

Together, they lit Millie's tea candles, already on the tables. They ushered in Dorothy Dodd, the high school music teacher, scheduled to be the nightly entertainment. Dorothy warmed up her fingers by playing the top piece of what seemed a nearly endless supply of sheet music piled beside Ruby's new Baldwin piano.

It was a busy night, a sparkling night. Music swelled through the room. Voices added a harmony to Dorothy's piano melodies. Glasses were raised. Toasts made. Merriment shared.

Ida and Ruby began to deliver prime rib dinners to their guests, placing the silver-trimmed dishes (reminiscent of the dishes Ruby had eaten from on long train rides) beside champagne flutes.

"Here we go," Ruby said, freezing mid-air when she realized she was about to serve this particular dinner to Nick Pendleton.

The same Nick Pendleton who worked with Roy Weber across the street.

Ruby's eyes darted about the interior of her supper club.

"He's not here," Nick told her.

Ruby offered a crooked smile. "Too bad he couldn't join us."

"Is it?"

The question set her off-balance, darkening her evening.

But Ida gave her a look that instructed her to simply carry on.

Ida. Ruby felt her cheeks turning the same shade as her name. "I grew up with Ida. She and my aunt, and…" she tried to explain.

"…and Timothy," Nick finished.

"I didn't think anyone remembered that."

"It's part of why Betty convinced me to sell the place. We'd always been warned to stay away from the pond, as kids. Granddad took the old bench away, made sure nobody'd come to skate anymore. Betty doesn't remember the skating at all, I don't think. Too young, maybe. I do a little. Almost seems like a dream, like something that was never real."

"It was, though," Ruby said softly. "And it was wonderful."

Nick eyed her a moment. "You know, we…" He tossed his head, as though to shake off whatever he was about to say. "Anyway, I'm here for your opening." He smiled.

Ruby smiled back, placing his dinner in front of him.

"Ida," Ruby hissed, pulling her into the kitchen.

"What in the world—?"

"Nick is here." She positioned Ida to see through the kitchen window, into the dining area. "What is he doing? Is he reporting back to Roy?"

"You think Roy sent a spy? And that it's *Nick*?"

"You don't think Nick would do it?"

"I think he'd be pretty bad at it. Nick's the family bumbler. Betty likes to call him the big lead assembly operator over at Chevrolet, but he's been nothing but a bouncer. From one failed attempt to another. Betty makes Roy take him in when the store even thinks about getting a little busy. Think those commissions are pretty inflated."

"But if he sees you..."

"What, he's going to tell on me?"

"Aren't you worried? He could get you fired."

Ida snorted a laugh. "Didn't you *ever* listen to that aunt of yours? What'd she say about enemies?"

Ruby's head spun through all the stray bits of wisdom her aunt had tried to impart on her. "That she...that...she lost her enemies when she made them her friends."

Ida offered a sly smile.

"What did you do?"

Ida held her hands out from her sides. "Young boys get into all sorts of trouble. Sometimes, they just need a little rescue."

Ruby tried to find comfort in it, but so much still felt off. She raced back out into the dining area, where she quickly stepped on her hairdresser's toe. When the hairdresser shrieked, Ruby skittered to the side, spilling a glass of champagne on Dorothy, the music teacher-slash-pianist.

"Sorry, sorry," Ruby said, trying to laugh it off.

But all she could feel were Nick's eyes.

Across Ruby's dining room, prime rib was devoured. Tables were pushed back and a dance floor cleared.

Ruby and Ida toasted their good work as the guests enjoyed a surprising (but somehow, they all agreed, perfect) dessert of homemade marshmallows and hot cocoa.

As the evening wound down, plates were collected, hugs were exchanged, and well-wishes were given.

"It's gonna be a hit, Rubes," Walter told her. "A hit!" as he placed his hat on his head and stepped into the starry night.

Slowly, the room emptied.

Until there was only Nick.

"Waiting for a second plate, Mr. Pendleton?" Ruby asked.

"Wouldn't mind one bit." He offered a grin and swayed in his chair.

One thing was clear; he didn't need another drink. She'd forgotten how many champagnes she'd brought him, and a small squat glass with half-melted cubes sat in front of him. What else had he been served? Some other stronger cocktail?

"I came by myself," he said.

"Yes. I know."

"I came by *myself*," he repeated, tilting his head to glare at Ruby in such a way as to warn her not to interrupt him this time. "Because I knew Roy wouldn't want to. I knew he'd try to talk me out of it. Or if he did come, I'd wind up seeing this place through his eyes. I didn't want that. I wanted to make up my own mind."

Ruby glanced to the side, at Ida. She shrugged, in a fake-innocent way. She'd served him that glass (or maybe more than one glass) of whatever that was in front of Nick. And she'd done it on purpose.

Ruby knew she was about to find out why.

"It's going to be wonderful, Ruby," Nick said, clutching his fork. "Or, it will be, if Roy doesn't get his way."

His face clouded as he fell back in his chair. It was right there, now, within reach: Nick's confession, loosened by the truth serum Ida had served.

"What is it?" Ruby pressed.

"You know what it is. He's bet against you."

Ruby sighed and sat in the chair opposite Nick. A small two-seater. Next to the window. The same place where she and Timothy had shared afternoons together. Back then, that very same spot had felt brimming with excitement and hope and all the love in a boy's bright blue eyes. It was a place of trust. Of no hesitancy. Sitting in the same spot, years later, staring at Nick, she felt suspicion. Fear. The need for a few protective walls.

"I would certainly rather not have an enemy across the street," Ruby admitted. "But I spent an entire career balancing on my toes. I suppose I can continue to do that a little longer."

Nick smiled, using his napkin to wipe sweat from his forehead. "I like you, Ruby. You're tough."

He started to push himself away from the table, as though to leave. But it didn't make her feel any less unsteady.

"Tougher than my sister, I'd say."

Ruby's skin tightened. A rash of goosebumps spread.

"Look, it's none of my business," Nick went on. "It's their marriage, not mine. And I'm not saying he's—*cruel*. Right? He loves her. I know that. She loves him. They're good together. But the way he sees her. Sees all of you, I guess. It's just—the horrible part is that I don't think I ever would have noticed if my sister hadn't been his wife. You know?"

"I understand," Ruby said. "More than you think, maybe."

"At least you have a sign."

Ruby frowned. A sign? From Timothy? She'd like nothing less. But where was it coming from? She swiveled in her seat.

"The sign," Nick repeated, pointing at the unlit neon leaning against a far wall. Her name looked enormous to her, suddenly.

"Oh. Right." She remembered how she'd felt when the crew from the sign company had guided that sign inside. How it had looked like a declaration. A bit like planting her flag to mark her territory.

"It belongs here. Your name belongs here."

After a pause, he moaned, "Why'd you have to pump your own gas?" Nick's eyes grew distant and he moved his jaw back and forth, almost like he was trying not to cry.

Ruby burst out laughing.

"I really don't know why you think it's funny."

"Because it is. That's so arbitrary and silly."

"Don't you get it, though? It's just a symptom. The pumping gas."

"Of what, though? A woman owner?"

"Yes. A woman—"

"But Millie owns that craft store."

"No. That's where you're wrong," Nick told her. The fog seemed to have lifted a bit from his eyes. "Her husband owns that craft store. He manages the books, does the hiring, the advertising..."

"So it's that I've gone into business on my own."

"And you've got *this* place. Not some yarn

store."

"Too masculine? Because it's sort of bar-like? The supper club thing isn't helping to tone that down a bit?"

"No, it's worse."

Ruby frowned.

"Have you ever looked at Roy? I mean really looked at him?"

Ruby wasn't sure what he meant. What was there to see? A middle-aged man, doing well in his life.

"Would you be surprised by the fact that his watch is 24-karat gold? That he has his shirts monogrammed and sent to Graham's Department Store on special order? Do you know that he has folks over for shrimp cocktail so he can show off the slides of his latest family vacation?"

"What does that have to do—"

"He's a man who thrives on adoration."

"But I'm not in competition with an electronics store."

"But you are. Because of the kind of man Roy is. Aren't you listening? He's respected by the community. Looked up to because he's the guy who sells the most modern thing around. Funny, isn't it? I mean, since he's so old-fashioned himself. The way he thinks.

"Now, though? You're bringing something far more modern here. Don't you see?" He gestured clumsily around the building. "You've brought New York. That's a real threat. For years, he could kind of act like he had the flashiest business in town. But once everybody finds out about this place? He won't be number one anymore. You're selling an experience. The kind of thing you don't get in some store."

Ruby glanced up at Ida, who nodded once. It was all true. Ruby was dealing a blow to Roy's ego.

"I just wish..." Nick slumped into his chair. "Look, like I said, he's not all bad. He's good to their kids, and he's done so much for Sullivan. Gives me work when I need it. Maybe that makes it worse. Because he's not just a black hat. He's not going around like some kind of Scrooge. But man, why *can't* Betty drive a car? Huh?"

Ruby shook her head, indicating she had no answer.

"I wish somebody would deal the guy a real blow. Just once."

And he thought Ruby could. That was the other half of it.

"You like to gamble, Nick?" she asked.

He shrugged. "On occasion."

"Bet on the fights?"

"Now and then."

"How about making Roy literally bet against me?"

"You really think Roy needs any more incentive—"

Ruby held up her hand to silence him. "Maybe I think you do. Maybe, if you had something at risk or something to win, you'd help interfere with what Roy's got up his sleeve. If the stakes are high enough, maybe it'll make you get a few Sullivanites on your side."

Nick thought a moment. "I like you, Ruby," he finally said. "You lay it all out on the line."

Ruby glanced at Ida, who grinned at her in a knowing way.

Nick held out his hand to Ruby.

They shook on it, sealing their own deal.

~

RUBY may have spent an entire career maintaining grace and balancing on her toes, but suddenly, the day after her soft opening, she was an utter klutz. She broke a beer mug and two martini glasses in a two-minute time frame. She bruised her hip as she attempted to race around the edge of the bar. She tripped over the cord on her Motorola clock radio upstairs.

She was nervous. And suspicious. It was the suspicion, she knew, that had set her off-balance.

But she also had a neon sign to ensure got hung. Which meant that she paraded about, down the sidewalk, swinging her silver bell door decoration all over again.

Nick and Roy emerged, as did the curls of smoke from their Pall Malls. Ruby shook her door ringer even harder, calling attention to the sign going back over her door, wordlessly asking Nick to remember the bet she wanted him to place.

She wanted Nick on her side. He seemed to know that. But would he buck Roy now that he was sober?

Her work crew flicked on the neon; she cheered when it washed a red glow against the sky. *Ruby's Place.*

Ruby thought she caught Nick watching through the front window of Weber's. That her shout had drawn him.

She paid the crew, replaced her checkbook, slammed her finger in the desk drawer, and was just about to head upstairs for the night when her phone rang behind the bar. She raced to answer, but it gave her an odd, apprehensive feeling. Nobody called on her work phone. Not yet, anyway.

"Hello?" she croaked, digging a nail into the curly cord stretching from the receiver.

"Ruby. It's me. Nick."

"Nick?" Ruby turned toward the front window, to find a man waving at her from the phone booth outside Weber Electronics.

"He took the bait, Ruby," Nick hissed. "Roy. Listen. While we were outside watching that sign of yours go up, he started talking about you. Acted like he'd never met you—like he'd forgotten he'd talked to you. I knew he was just trying to dig for info, find out if I'd gone inside and what it was like—what *you* were really like. Anyway, he bet me that you'd never get open. Said he'd take Betty, me, and a guest all out to dinner at your place on Christmas Eve. But not just once, oh, no. That guy's so deluded, he told me that if you didn't get open, he'd take us all out to your place every Christmas Eve for the rest of his life. Can you believe that?"

Ruby felt her stomach turn over. "Awfully steep," she murmured.

"Aw, come on. The guy doesn't have a chance. You already held your soft opening. I mean, you're right there! It's a done deal. You're as good as open right now. Why would he make such a dumb bet?"

"Nick," Ruby said, worry making her skin feel instantly tight, "do you think—"

But the front door of Weber's flew open, and Nick glanced behind his shoulder. "Gotta go, Ruby. Talk soon."

Ruby's ear filled with a dial tone as Nick slammed the receiver back down.

He rushed from the payphone as Roy put a

cigarette in his mouth, cupped the end to protect it from a wintry gust, and lit it.

Roy frowned as he slipped his gold lighter back into his pocket.

Ruby could hear their voices, muffled. Roy giving him some sort of grief. Something about spending too many dimes on some girlfriend. Nick telling him to *back off, why don't you?*

Ruby tried to find comfort in Nick lying about who he'd had on the phone. But when Roy laughed, so did Nick. In a way that said the two of them were pals. They took off together, Nick acting in front of Roy like he'd never been on Ruby's side at all.

15.

THE chamber of commerce printings showed up as scheduled, first thing the very next morning, with a *thump* on Ruby's sidewalk. She raced outside, even before she collected the two wheeler she'd purchased with the intention of being able to help move her liquor deliveries from the back door to the storage room. Ruby was not one to simply point and direct others, after all. She was a worker. On the sidewalk, Ruby attacked the stack of printings she had promised to place inside her door and on the edge of the bar. Anywhere her customers would be sure to see them and grab a copy for themselves.

She snatched the top copy with eagerness. On the cover, around the picture of a lit-up tree on the square, red and green letters spelled out, "Sullivan's Best Businesses Invite You to Enjoy Christmas. Eat,

Shop, and Be Merry!"

Heart speeding up, Ruby flipped through it page after page.

Then flipped back-to-front.

Frowning, she tried again.

She searched the index.

She looked under "Restaurants" and "Bars" and "Clubs."

Fuming, she raced across the street, straight into Weber Electronics.

"What is this?" she bellowed, rattling the pages.

Roy shook his head, removing his reading glasses and tossing them on some sort of paperwork he had spread out on the counter before him.

"Why am I not in this? I was counting on this!"

"I know," Roy said evenly.

On the opposite side of the room, Nick watched with wide, fearful eyes.

"Playing dirty," Ruby thundered. This was why Roy'd been so willing to make that bet with Nick. "What do you think all this is going to accomplish? Huh? I *bought* the place."

"You need a big Christmas season. All season long. Can't waste a day. At this point, you're running out of cash. I know that."

"That's your goal? To dig me a hole."

"No."

"What, then?"

"I'm going to make your life miserable."

"You already are."

"Not yet, I'm not. True misery comes from failure."

"I'll just keep on going. Haven't you been paying attention? The deliveries, the paint, all those jobs that got finished anyway."

Roy took a few steps forward. "The screws have yet to completely tighten."

"My opening is already right around the corner."

"Oh, honey," he said. "You're on your way out of town. Nobody's coming. Not for your official opening. Don't you know by Christmas Eve, you'll be gone?"

"No, I won't. I'll ignore you. I'll work around you."

Roy chuckled, crossing his arms over his chest. "I'll crank up the heat."

"Until what?"

"Until you break, darlin'." Roy winked. "It's what you women are good at. Breakin'."

16.

RUBY didn't get out the rest of the day. Not after her confrontation with Roy. Not to the diner and not to Millie's Craft Store. She didn't buy herself a newspaper. She didn't pick up her cleaning.

She was angry. The kind of angry that she didn't want to show Sullivan. Not if she didn't want them believing Roy Weber had the upper hand.

Which, let's face it, he did. Ruby knew now that he'd been behind it all: every delay, every permit that didn't arrive on time. For the sign, even. He had to have been the one who had called the neon company away, too quickly to secure her first sign. But who else had he paid to lay blockades in Ruby's path?

Did the men of Sullivan even need to be paid off? How many of them simply wanted to be on Roy's good side? Had Jake at Jake's Appliances told Roy about her clock radio? Bragged (or tattled) that she'd made her purchase somewhere other than Roy's? Were the men here in the habit of following along with whatever he said? How many let his opinions also be theirs?

Roy had been the main force behind the depletion of Ruby's pocketbook. If there hadn't been so many delays, she wouldn't be so strapped right now.

And that infuriated her. Terrified her.

She would get open. No matter what Roy had in mind. But who would come? None of the men who wanted to remain on Roy's good side. None of his fellow Shriners or the city council or the members of the chamber of commerce.

What about the fellow business owners she had treated at her soft opening? Would they show? Would they really spread the word of her prime rib and marshmallows? Or would that be considered crossing Roy?

How alone was Ruby, really?

How true was Roy's prediction? She was down to her last dime. If no one came for her official opening, *would* she be closed by Christmas? Could everything really crumble that fast? After so much work?

Roy sure thought so. Even if she did technically open, he'd never have to make good on that bet with Nick. Not if she already had to shut up shop before the new year.

Ruby flicked her switch. The red neon glow filled the darkening twilight.

The street in front of Ruby's Place was mostly empty. The diner down the block was still seating people, but for the most part, "Closed" signs were all turned toward the curbs.

Ruby was exhausted. It took so much out of her to cook up that much hatred for one person.

And yet, as tired as she was, she was also having trouble stopping.

She wondered how long she should leave her neon sign on. Just a few hours? What was the point? She wasn't even open yet. How much would her electric bill be? She hated having money hold her back on anything, because it only made her think all over again of Roy and the delays he'd caused. A fresh round of hatred exploded through her chest.

She walked to her old spot. The one beside the front window. The one she had shared with Timothy. "What good was it?" she asked. All of this fighting, this struggling. If her success wasn't even entirely up to her?

She glared at the red glow coming from her sign.

"Yeah," she grumbled. "Some sign."

As she stared, the door flew open across the

street. Roy Weber emerged, in his wool topcoat. Nick was nowhere in sight; probably already at the Chevrolet plant. Ruby's eyes narrowed as she watched Roy head toward his car. A brand-new Oldsmobile. But the wind lifted his hat from his head. A black hat. With a red hatband around the center.

Ruby red, Ruby thought sourly. *He shouldn't get to wear red, anyway. I'm the one who should get red. Blow, hat, blow.*

She smiled, watching him chase after it. Without warning, the wind changed direction, sending the hat tumbling out of Roy's fingers again. He took a step backward, slamming against a lamppost. The post rattled all the way up; the aluminum star attached near the top swayed once, twice, then broke free. It tumbled, whacking Roy on the crown of his head.

Ruby barked a laugh. Served him right, she thought.

Roy's hand went to the top of his head. He staggered forward a few steps.

Ruby's smile started to fade.

Roy drooped, closer and closer to the pavement.

"Oh, you've got to be kidding me," she grumbled.

Roy passed out, falling into the street.

She burst outside. "Roy?" Ruby shouted. "Roy!"

Ruby dropped down beside him, put her hands

on his shoulder. "Roy?" She leaned closer. "Roy!"

But he was out cold.

Behind her, the glow of her sign intensified; out of nowhere, the red tint began to wash over Roy's face.

Ruby swiveled, glancing over her shoulder. This sign wasn't malfunctioning, too, was it? It wasn't burning too hot, too bright?

Before she could make sense of it, a cardinal fluttered by, dropping something from his beak. Nest-making material? Did birds even make nests this time of year? Only, it wasn't a twig or a clump of fur or a pine sprig; instead, a piece of paper floated to the ground beside her.

"I lose my enemies each time I make them my friends," she found written on the page. She looked about her for the source. But the street was empty.

Except for the face in the front window of her building.

Ruby gasped; that pink-cheeked young face of a boy. That familiar face. The notebook in one of his hands. He raised his empty hand—which had a pencil woven between a few fingers—in a wave.

When Ruby blinked, he disappeared.

But she still held that piece of paper.

It was another sign. Ruby was sure of it.

Timothy had been right before, and he was right about this now.

She shoved the piece of notebook paper in her pants pocket and lurched toward the nearby phone booth. The same Nick had used the day before to call her.

Ruby begged the operator, "Hurry. I need help."

17.

"HE'S waking up," Betty sighed, putting her hand to her chest in relief.

Roy's eyes fluttered open. His lips parted in surprise and his legs began to move about under the blankets as he struggled to make sense of it all.

"Sir?" a doctor asked. "Do you know where you are?"

"No, no," Roy said, but clearly it was sinking in: he was in a hospital bed. In a hospital gown. In a private room. And the room was full of people. His eyes bounced across them all: a couple of doctors in their white coats; a cluster of nurses in their aprons and their little white hats; Betty, looking upset in the chair at his bedside; Nick at his feet; a strange man in an overcoat with a press badge; a police officer; and (*ye gods*, his expression seemed to say) Ruby herself.

"You hit your head," Nick told him.

"One of those lamppost snowflakes fell and hit you on the head," Ruby corrected.

Roy reached up, wincing when his fingertips found the sore spot.

"You were out cold for quite some time," one of the doctors said, shining a light in his eyes and lifting up one of his eyelids.

Roy squirmed out of the doctor's grip.

"We were so worried, sweetie," Betty said. "But don't worry, the kids are with my mom."

"How did I—how did—"

"Ruby called for an ambulance," Betty told him.

"Well," Ruby said, "I had to help. I mean, after everything you've done for me."

"How's that?" Roy asked, glaring at her.

Ruby glared back, the two of them recognizing, wordlessly, that everything Roy had done in relation to Ruby had been less than helpful. Had been an attempt to destroy all she was creating.

Roy's glare had an added question in it: *What's going on here?*

"Ruby told the nurses all about it, sir," the doctor informed him, slipping his pen light into the breast pocket on his white coat.

"And then we called the newspaper," one of the

nurses chimed in.

"The news?"

"Yes," the nurse went on. "Ruby there, she said that she wished everyone in town could find out about what you did. She asked if any of us knew how to get to the newspaper. This is one of those feel-good stories that are perfect for the news this time of year! A kindhearted man, looking out for the new woman in town. Acting like a regular Santa Claus where she's concerned. And of course, Mary's son-in-law..."—here, she turned to point to another nurse, who smiled and waved at Roy—"...just happens to be a journalist! So lucky. I was so glad Ruby asked."

"I've been looking for a way to thank you publicly for so long," Ruby admitted.

Again, the glare at Ruby.

At this point, she was having an awfully hard time keeping a grin from breaking through.

"Yes. The way you saved Ms. Westbrook," the reporter said, clicking his pen.

"Saved?"

"*You* know," Betty said. "How those jealous men have been after Ruby right from the start. Since she moved to town. How they've been delaying everything. Her permits. Her deliveries. They may have even made sure her sign would fall." She nodded once, her mouth curled in a *bet you can't believe that* sort of manner.

"I mean, I thought, well..." Betty fidgeted, digging a thumb into the top button on her dress. "Maybe even I thought Ruby was pushing the limits. Asking for trouble. But *you*..." Betty tilted her head, in awe of her forward-thinking husband. "You knew better. All along." She leaned forward to squeeze his hand again.

"And there was an attempt, isn't that right?" the police officer asked. "As Ms. Westbrook was leaving her building? A whole group coming after her?"

"But I didn't see any faces," Ruby reminded him.

"Did you, sir? See any? I know it would have been hard," the officer said.

"I—"

"After all, you were more interested in getting to me. Like I told the officer here," Ruby went on. "Making sure I was okay. And in the midst of it all, that metal star fell, hitting you on the head. Of course, that was enough to send the men all scattering in different directions. I don't even know if those were actually Sullivan men, or if they came in from another town. Word having really started to spread about my place."

"Honey," Betty sighed. "Taking on all those men at once. How many of them, did you say, Ruby?"

"Oh, five or six. Maybe seven."

"Seven!" Betty cooed.

"You're a regular hero, sir," the reporter declared, reaching out to shake his hand. "I'd love to highlight you in the paper."

"Be sure you get it in your article how Roy has been my hero from the start," Ruby pressed. "You know, my establishment was supposed to be in the annual chamber of commerce printing. A clerical error kept it out. And when I pointed that out to Roy, he insisted on a special edition, all to highlight my own Ruby's Place."

"You didn't!" Betty squealed.

"Quite generous of you, sir," the reporter said, snapping a picture of Roy before he could refuse.

"Yes. Well. It was nothing," Roy stammered.

"Nothing," one of the nurses repeated. She nudged another of her fellow nurses with her elbow. "You hear that? *Nothin'*, he says." The two shook their heads at Roy's modesty.

"What he means is," Nick piped up, sneaking a glance at Ruby, "we'll all be at Ruby's Place on Christmas Eve. He wants the rest of Sullivan to join us, too."

18.

"HOW are the marshmallows coming?" Ruby asked Ida as she burst into the kitchen.

"Moving as fast as I can," Ida responded, wiping sweat from her forehead. "Is traffic slowing down?"

"Not yet," Ruby admitted.

"Good night," Ida sighed. "Still coming, this late on Christmas Eve?"

They were. So many of them that when Ruby attempted to respond, she was drowned out by the sounds of the piano and the voices, all coming together to sing "Joy to the World."

Ruby tried to reach for the tray of marshmallows, preparing to give them a quick toast that would turn them even more gooey and irresistible.

But Ida stopped her. "Look who just showed up," she told Ruby, pushing her toward the window to the dining area.

Ruby craned her neck to get a glimpse of the area near the entrance. "Roy," she said with a smile. In what appeared to be a new suit, Betty on his arm. Nick followed, taking his date's coat and hanging it near the entrance.

"Some deal you worked there," Ida told her.

"All because you reminded me what my aunt used to say," Ruby told a sweaty-faced Ida. That, and the piece of paper that had floated down to her. Timothy, she'd thought when she was young, had managed to hear everything. It had only seemed right, when she'd seen that piece of paper, that he would have heard her aunt's favorite saying, too. At the hospital, when the emergency room crew had zipped Roy off to be examined, Ruby had slipped her hand into her pants pocket, only to find it empty. Had the paper fallen in her scramble to help Roy into the ambulance? Or as she'd raced into the hospital?

Had it ever truly existed?

Ida grinned. "You think you really did make him your friend?"

"Well. He's going to keep up the appearance of being my friend," Ruby said. "He sure has benefited from the town believing it."

In fact, after the story had run in the paper, the women had swarmed to Weber Electronics. They'd come not just for Christmas gifts, but to deliver baskets of baked goods. Candy canes. Homemade ornaments. They'd come to fawn over him, their civic leader who had gone beyond the call of duty.

Ethel had even made an appearance at the shop. "Oh," she'd said, tossing a hand at Nick's sales pitch. "I'm too old to care for any of these doodads. I came to thank Roy for helping my good friend Ruby." She'd grasped Roy's hands in hers, saying, "You're a good man," in a way that had clearly reverberated through him. Did she really mean that? Or, if Ethel was such a close friend of Ruby's, had she known all along the story in the paper was a lie? Was she telling him to be a better man?

The questions had flashed across Roy's face as they'd stared into each other's eyes, and again as she'd left the store.

Roy'd propped a hand on his hip and scratched the top of his head. "What?" he'd grumbled at Nick, who had simply shrugged innocently. But Nick had worn a grin, too—the kind that showed how much he'd enjoyed that particular visit.

Walter'd jaywalked, dodging the front fender of an Edsel in order to hop onto the sidewalk in front of Weber Electronics. "You must believe what I always have," he'd told Roy as he shook his hand. "That Ruby's is a sure thing."

The other men of Sullivan had watched all this attention, and they'd begun to think maybe Roy was onto something. Amongst themselves, they talked about how it must have been his grand scheme all along: to give Ruby roadblocks in order to get the credit for taking those roadblocks away.

Regardless, they'd all learned long ago how handy it was to have such a powerful Sullivan figure on their sides. And so they'd slapped him on the shoulder or tipped their hats. "Quite a story in that paper," they'd said. "Well-deserved, well-deserved."

More importantly, perhaps, they'd witnessed the female attention that was being heaped on Roy (a married man, no less, who could not take full advantage of their swoony looks), and had felt their chests swell with jealousy. Admiration. Longing. Suddenly, they, too, were supportive of Ms. Westbrook's endeavors. The liquor distributor donated some extra crates of rum. The grocer brought by some extra staples. The man who had installed the gas line showed up to double-check his work.

All while making sure the women of Sullivan took note of their efforts.

"I'll be here," they'd all promised, as Ruby had prepared for her official opening. "Wouldn't miss this holiday season for the world."

And they'd kept those promises. They had

come. Many brought their families. Others sought Walter out first, before even glancing at Ruby's menu. Slathering him in compliments. Why, he could see a good business idea a hundred miles away. (All, Ruby'd figured, an attempt to butter him up before coming to sit on the opposite side of his desk at the Bank of Sullivan, asking him to see the merits of their own business plan. Asking him to agree to help fund it.) But once business—or the business of being seen, at least—had been handled, they'd settled in for the evening. They'd exchanged gifts and sung carols.

They had, in fact, come more than once. They'd made arrangements for office Christmas parties. They'd brought friends and visitors from out of town. Ruby's became a first stop after picking a guest up from the train station.

Yes, something had happened, as the days had inched closer and closer to Christmas. Something far more powerful than the chamber of commerce Ruby's Place edition. The men who had come for show, obligatory smiles on their faces, had slowly begun to soften. Their eyes had begun to sparkle as they'd entered. They'd come for Ida's mouth-watering recipes. They'd come for Dorothy's piano music. They'd come for cocktails and conversation, for the special feeling that seemed to fill the building beneath the crystal chandeliers.

Frankly, they'd begun to like the place.

They'd come, in short, because the entirety of the building felt like Christmas. Warm and happy and hopeful. Snow trickled to the ground outside, sparkling in the red glow of Ruby's neon sign. And somehow, through Ruby's window, it seemed sweet and pure. Sitting there, in a special setting, as the holiday closed in, it had been easy to open their hearts.

Just as easy as it had once been for Ruby to open her own heart to Timothy, sitting right in that very building. She had often wondered, as she'd delivered plates and welcomed her guests and mixed cocktails, if that unafraid kind of love was still there. If it had somehow seeped into the bricks.

All she'd known for certain was that when she was inside her building, she didn't feel flooded with memories of better times gone by. Instead, she felt like she was at the beginning of her story again. She was no longer a retired has-been ballerina with sore feet. She was young; she could dance on the sidewalk and skate across the pond. She could fall into a snowdrift and flap her arms and legs. Her heart had rewound the clock.

And now, here he was. Roy. On Christmas Eve, no less.

He'd already agreed he'd show, of course. But to see him was another matter entirely. It filled her with the pleasant sensation of having triumphed.

Ruby raced to greet him.

"Well, here I am," he grumbled.

As Betty, Nick, and Nick's date drifted off to find a table in the midst of the commotion, Roy leaned closer to Ruby and confessed, "Listen, lady, I'm still not sure about this thing you've got going here. But I gotta ask: what made you so sure I'd go along with your story? The one about me being some sort of great hero defender?"

In truth, Ruby'd banked on Nick being right about him. That Roy was, above all else, addicted to adoration. Instead, she said, "I knew you'd never let your wife down."

He shot her a disbelieving look.

But he also offered her a half grin.

"Betty and Nick insisted we bring you a gift," he said.

"Oh, yeah?"

"Yeah. It's outside."

19.

"ARE we doing it now?" Betty squealed, gathering up their coats again. "I thought we were saving it."

Roy only shrugged into his topcoat. "...get this thing over with..." Ruby thought she heard him grumble.

"Gloves, hon," Betty told Roy. "It's a cold one."

Roy complied, but only after lighting a cigarette.

Nick put his hands over Ruby's eyes. Together, he and Betty helped her through the door. "Straight ahead, Ruby," Betty cooed. "Right this way."

"Ready for the big reveal?" Nick asked.

Beside her, Roy grunted.

"On the count of three," Betty said. "One, two...ta-da!"

Nick pulled his fingers back, and Ruby fought to catch her breath.

"The bench," Ruby said. "From the pond."

"Told you she'd recognize it," Nick told his sister.

"I swear, I thought it was just some crummy old relic," Betty said.

"No," Ruby said, sliding onto the bench. "It's fantastic."

"Ida knew where it'd be. In the old shed," Nick explained. "You should be sure to thank her."

"I will," Ruby murmured. Then added, "For so many things."

They all stood beside her a moment, somewhat awkwardly. Ruby sniffed back a few tears.

"Come on, hon," Betty finally said, breaking the tension as she reached for Ruby's arm. "It's so cold out here."

But Ruby shook her head. She tugged at her own coat—she was wearing a looser, far less fussy coat these days than the one she'd worn when she arrived back in town on that Christmas Eve three years ago. This one was a winter white with a large, swooping collar she could pull up like a scarf around her throat. "I'd like to stay a while," she said, turning her face away so that Betty couldn't see the tears now escaping her eyes.

Betty could surely hear them in her voice, though. She patted Ruby's shoulder. "All right, dear. But don't stay too long, okay?"

Ruby nodded and listened as the Webers and

Pendletons all slipped back inside.

The bench was somewhat worse for wear, with rust along the edges of the metal legs, and red paint flaking off the wooden slats. This was the same paint, though, that had touched Timothy. And the younger her.

She let her fingers, pink from cold, run along a wrinkling section of paint. A few bits tumbled off, flittering toward the ground like snowflakes.

In the distance, Ruby could make out a faint train whistle. The last one before the holiday, pulling into the station.

Ruby smiled, smelling the cold snow in the air, and knowing that trains were behind her. As were lonely Christmas Eves. This was the first of a new era. One in which Ruby was truly, officially home.

Behind Ruby, the door opened.

"Hey."

When she turned toward the gruff voice, there he was. Again.

"Roy."

"Yeah, well, Ida in there wanted me to bring this to you." He held a champagne flute. When Ruby accepted it, he added, "And this."

Ruby smiled at the scrapbook.

"She said you have to find something to put in it before the night is over."

"I bet she did."

Roy continued to stare at her. "I looked," he said, pointing at the scrapbook.

"And?"

He shrugged. "Not bad."

She scooted to the side, making room for him. He hesitated, but then seemed to nod in agreement at someone on the other side of the front window. Betty, maybe? One of the Sullivan women who had become his fans, almost as though he were a local version of Paul Newman or Bill Haley?

At any rate, he turned away from the window and sat beside her, in the same way a man might sit beside a tiger.

"Relax," she grumbled, offering him a sip of her champagne.

There they were, the two of them on the bench that had once held every single person in Sullivan. That had welcomed them to the Pendleton pond, where they'd taken to the ice to laugh and play and drink in the feeling of utter freedom.

Here the bench would remain, to welcome once again the people of Sullivan. To guarantee that stepping inside Ruby's Place would bring back the open-hearted ways of youth. To reassure them that life continued on, offering new gifts, even after something lovely had come to its end.

Did Roy feel that? Would he allow himself to feel it? She wasn't sure.

But he did take a sip of the champagne.

"Why are you looking at me like that?" he asked. "You got something else cooking, Westbrook? 'Cause you and me, we're square."

"No, actually, we're never going to be completely square."

Roy frowned. "How's that?"

"You had a bet with Nick."

"How'd you know—"

"A bet that, if you lost, would have you coming here on Christmas Eve *every single year*. Isn't that right?"

Roy's face drooped.

"Looks like you're my very first regular," Ruby said, as Roy growled and slammed a fist on his leg.

She laughed, because she had him. He couldn't come back at her, not if he wanted to maintain his new reputation.

Disgusted, he handed her drink back. And he stomped inside her building.

Above, the streetlights glimmered against the silver-toned snowflakes.

As the music and the voices continued to bleed through the window behind her, Ruby pulled a small notebook from the pocket of her coat.

"Hello?" she wrote.

Ever so slowly, the ground began to change. No longer were her feet positioned on a sidewalk, but buried in two inches of snow. And her ears filled with the sound of skates scraping the ice. One person after another, flying past.

"Ruby!" came the shout.

When she raised her head, she saw her namesake aunt, holding her arm out as she coasted by.

"You look like a hood ornament," she croaked, overcome with emotion.

Her aunt laughed.

A young man stopped in front of her. His feet began to swirl. When he was done, he'd written in the ice, "Glad?"

Ruby let out a sound that was not quite a laugh and not quite a cry. "Yes," she signed. "Glad."

He sat beside her. On her notebook, she wrote, "It smells like snow."

Timothy smiled; he'd written the same thing to her the first day they'd gone to Frankie's together.

Then, she scrawled, "How do I repay you?"

He wiggled his fingers, asking for her pencil. When she handed it to him, he wrote, "I used to reserve your seat for you. Now, you reserve this seat for me."

"I will," Ruby whispered. "I promise."

She crumpled the top sheet of her notebook paper into her pocket, acting too quickly to see for sure if the page had been filled with two different styles of handwriting.

She leaned back against the bench, which was perched, yet again, on the sidewalk. The pond had disappeared. A car drove down the street, offering a quick honk of hello at her.

Ruby waved.

And still, behind her, the merry sounds of Christmas Eve carried on.

The click of footsteps drew her to standing. A cluster of new customers nearly skipped as they made their way down the sidewalk.

She reached for the door, holding it open. "Welcome to Ruby's Place," she said, ushering the couples inside two by two.

The words rippled outward, playing a melody as they pinged against the snowflake decorations.

Real snowflakes began to swirl; Ruby opened the scrapbook, letting a few fall on the first blank page. She closed the book quickly, capturing them.

Her practical voice scolded her, telling her that was impossible. The same voice also insisted it was impossible for Timothy to have just been there, sitting beside her on the bench. But Ruby reminded her practical side that it never would have believed she'd get

Roy to come for Christmas Eve.

Miracles—even tiny ones—were built for Christmas.

She could have danced right there on the sidewalk, with no concern about what the rest of the world thought.

And that's exactly what she did. She danced, so that Timothy could hear her. One arm hugging her scrapbook to her chest, the other arcing gracefully over her head.

No matter what the years would bring her way, Ruby knew she'd never quit believing that Timothy was right here. In the glass and the brick, somehow. In the very air that tingled against her skin.

It *had* been important. It had been real love. A woman didn't have to convince herself that love existed. It just was. In a matter of moments.

She didn't have to convince herself now that Timothy had been guiding her all along. That he had brought her home. That he would continue to be there, right beside her—*Timothy's Place*.

Ruby twirled and she skipped. Her heart overflowed. When Ethel arrived for the evening, she would see a far different woman than she had first met in the lobby of the Grand. She would find a happy woman.

She'd find a woman who still danced.

Ruby knew, as the faces gathered in her front

window to watch, and as Timothy applauded from the bench outside, she would never quit believing that this building was actually her heart. The purest, youngest version of her heart.

She'd never quit believing that Ruby's Place was utter magic.

COME BACK TO *Ruby's*

Ruby's Story is the prequel to **The Ruby's Place Christmas Collection**, a four-book series about what became of Ruby's Place after she poured her last drink:

Book 1: Christmas at Ruby's

Book 2: I Remember You

Book 3: Sentimental Journey

Book 4: The Gift That Is Ruby's Place

Or, get the single-download full collection:

HOLLYSCHINDLER.COM
for details.

Stay tuned for additional installments.

HOLLY SCHINDLER

Holly Schindler is a critically acclaimed and award-winning author of books for readers of all ages. She believes nothing is quite as magical as storytelling.

She's currently drafting her next story (and also probably drinking too much coffee, and if it's the holidays, singing carols so loudly, even the neighbors can hear).

She wishes you a very happy holiday season, and invites you to view her full list of publications, subscribe to a newsletter or two, or get in touch at:

HOLLYSCHINDER.COM